A Podcast To Die For

A Costa Rica Beach Cozy Mystery

K.C. Ames

17th
STREET
BOOKS

About This Book

One of the most popular true crime podcasts comes to Mariposa Beach to record a podcast about the mysterious disappearance of an eccentric millionaire who was Benny Campos, client. Murder and mayhem ensue and Benny finds himself in a pickle as a prime suspect as Dana Kirkpatrick tries to figure out the truth about what's going on.

Chapter One

COSTA RICA HAD TWO SEASONS: wet and dry. Dana Kirkpatrick was sitting at the sales counter of her bookstore in Mariposa Beach watching the rain fall hard for its typical midafternoon deluge, which meant there weren't many customers willing to walk through the pounding rain to buy a book.

It was a perfect time for her to catch up to one of her favorite true crime podcasts: *What Really Happened?*

The host, Cheyenne Lively, was wrapping up the six-part series about a missing Maine woman. It was the focus of that podcast to deep-dive into cold cases of missing people or murder cases that the police could not solve.

Cheyenne Lively's track record was impressive. Not only did she deliver a binge-worthy podcast, but her investigations into these old cases had led to the capture of several murderers who had evaded justice for years, and had even exonerated a wrongfully convicted man.

Dana was listening to the final minutes of the podcast at her bookstore slash cafe, Books, Bagels, and Lattes, located in Ark Row—a small strip of less than a mile that was home to most

1

merchants of the small beach-town community of Mariposa Beach in the Guanacaste Province on the northern Pacific coast.

Dana owned and operated the bookstore side of the bookstore slash cafe. Her best friend in town, Mindy Salas, owned the cafe side of the slash with her husband, Leo Salas.

Even during the busy tourist season—known as the dry season—things were usually slower on the bookstore side. Most tourists had gone digital. They weren't beating down her door for a paperback. But the rainy season was the slowest time for all the vendors in Ark Row, who depended on tourists to make a living.

Dana always thought that the tourists milling around town during the rainy season were the savvy ones. They might have to endure a couple hours of heavy rain in the afternoon, but ended up with pretty nice weather before and after the rains.

There were many pluses to coming to Costa Rica during the wet season. All that rain put Costa Rica's majestic ecology into overdrive, showing off its verdant might like a peacock showing off its feathers.

The beaches were less crowded—way less people than during peak tourist months—and the prices of everything, from hotel rooms, yoga classes, and even restaurants dipped by fifteen to twenty percent during the rainy season. Dana thought it was the time to come, really.

For the merchants, the off-season was the window to enjoy the peacefulness of the small coastal town.

And Dana could overdose on podcasts and audiobooks.

Yep, Dana had a problem. She was hooked on true crime shows. And there seemed to be a nonstop supply of the stuff.

The pace of crime documentaries being released on the streaming channels was feverish and unrelenting. Then there were cable channels dedicated to true crime, and network television had its magazine shows like Dateline dedicated to providing the true crime junkie their fix.

But for all the mediums out there, podcasting was Dana's favorite. She enjoyed the audio storytelling component harking back to the days when radio was king. Listening to a podcast let her imagination do a lot of the heavy-lifting.

Dana could plop in her earbuds and listen to her favorite podcast while she cleaned the house, went out for a beach run, or even at work in her bookstore when business was slow.

Her love of true crime was enjoyed from a distance. She knew no one involved in a real-life true crime story. That was, until Cheyenne Lively dropped a teaser for her upcoming podcast series. Dana was listening, but she was multitasking as she clicked on her laptop, entering her latest book order for the store. When she heard Cheyenne Lively say the words "Costa Rica," she stopped multitasking, a tinge of excitement growing as she heard Cheyenne Lively's warm voice reverberating from her earbuds...

So join us, true crime fiends, on the next series of What Really Happened, which will bring you the puzzling story of Ed North, an eccentric multimillionaire from Florida who hopped on his Cessna airplane, which he himself piloted, en route to his ranch in the tropical paradise of Mariposa Beach, Costa Rica, only to vanish seven years ago. The police are stumped. And the rumor mill has been running rampant on this odd case, my true crime fiends.

The first and second wife battled over his millions of dollars, with the first wife pointing the finger at the younger second wife, accusing her of being involved in Ed's mysterious disappearance. And wife number two claims her innocence and points a finger at Ed North's alleged shady dealings down in Costa Rica, even questioning if he's really dead.

Is Ed North dead or alive? If he's dead, was he murdered? What really happened to Ed North? Join us next month for the latest investigation to find What Really Happened to Ed North down in Costa Rica.

Dana almost fell off the stool. She couldn't believe it. Cheyenne Lively's next podcast series was not only going to be about a true crime that occurred in Costa Rica, but right here in Mariposa Beach. *How exciting*, she thought as she plopped the earbuds out of her ears. That excitement was now morphing into curiosity. She hadn't heard about Ed North and his disappearance. She glanced toward the coffee shop side and saw Mindy Salas reviewing the day's receipts. Dana leaned over her store counter and shouted out toward her. "Hey, Mindy, that true crime podcast I was telling you about..."

"You have to be more specific. You're always listening to one of those podcasts," Mindy said.

"The one about missing and unsolved crimes."

"Is that the one with Wyoming Something?"

Dana laughed. "Wyoming? No, her name is Cheyenne. Cheyenne Lively, silly."

"Hey, Cheyenne is the capital of Wyoming. I was close."

"Okay, sure, you can have that one, but guess what?"

Mindy wasn't a fan of true crime or podcasts, so she shrugged her shoulders and gave Dana an indifferent look, showing she was fast losing interest in the conversation.

"Her next podcast will cover a crime that happened right here in Mariposa Beach."

Mindy's face now showed interest in the subject.

Mindy's husband, Leo, who ran the kitchen, popped his head out from his lair and asked, "Which crime is that?"

"Hon, we've talked about the eavesdropping," Mindy said.

"She's shouting from across the room. I think Big Mike could hear her without having to eavesdrop."

Dana blushed. Big Mike was the owner of Big Mike's Surf and Shop next door. He was a former pro big-wave surfer with a Mavericks surf competition under his belt. He now gave surfing lessons to tourists and rented just about anything needed to have an adventurous vacation around the beaches and rainforest near Mariposa Beach. From snorkeling gear, boogie boards, dive tanks, and ATVS—Big Mike had all the toys for the adrenaline-seeking tourists.

Dana ignored Leo's comment about her being loud wanting to know more about Ed North and what had happened to him in Mariposa Beach that would warrant a six-episode run on Cheyenne's podcast.

"It's about some eccentric millionaire that went missing. Ed North was his name," Dana said.

The mood changed quickly. Mindy and Leo's face changed in an instant from amused curiosity to dread. Like she had sucked the wind out of the place. Dana felt like she had passed gas in church. Mindy and Leo exchanged worried glances, saying nothing, but their silence spoke volumes.

"What? Do you guys know him? Share the dirt. What do you know?"

"Um, well. Benny never mentioned Ed North to you?" a nervous Mindy said, stammering.

"My Benny? No, why?"

Benny Campos was Dana's boyfriend. He had been her real estate attorney when she moved down to Mariposa Beach after inheriting a beautiful beach house known as Casa Verde close to town. One thing led to another, and although she had sworn off getting into a relationship so soon after her divorce, she and Benny became close, and they had become even closer in the past year since she moved down to Mariposa Beach, and were now in a committed, loving relationship. Benny made her happy, but the idea of a serious relationship still scared the living daylights out of her. She figured it was to be expected after the mess that was being married to a cheating scoundrel Silicon Valley tech bro like her ex.

"You should ask him about Ed North, honey," Mindy said.

"Ed was a nice dude. Weird as heck, but a nice guy. Could never tell he was millionaire, the way he dressed and carried himself. He was Benny's client when he went missing," Leo said.

Mindy looked at Leo as if to tell him telepathically to shut up about Ed North.

"Oh, jeez, really? I wonder if Cheyenne will want to interview Benny," Dana said.

"I would imagine she will, and I can guarantee you that Benny will not like it one bit," Leo said.

"I don't know. It might be fun," Dana said.

"Trust me, he won't like it," Leo said.

Dana gave him a puzzled look and Mindy launched her DEFCON 2 stare toward her husband.

"What? She's going to find out about all of it anyway," Leo said.

"Find out about what? So he had a client that went missing. I'm sure that's not uncommon for an attorney with many clients over their career," Dana said. She noticed her voice sounded defensive. And a counterargument popped in her head as well: *Oh, really? It's common for lawyers to have clients go missing?*

Mindy came toward Dana, looking like a concerned parent.

"Ed North's disappearance was big news around here years ago. It created a lot of havoc in Benny's life." Just as Mindy was telling Dana that, Doña Amada, an octogenarian and the unofficial leader of the old biddies in town known as the Gossip

Brigade, walked into the bookstore slash cafe, having overheard what Mindy had said.

"That's putting it lightly," Doña Amada said as she shook her wet umbrella, sending water droplets all over.

Dana, Mindy, and Leo turned their heads toward the old biddy, who seemed to have no filter for saying what popped into that hardened old skull of hers. Or if she ever had that internal filter, it had worn out long ago.

"What do you mean by that?" Dana asked.

Doña Amada smiled, knowing she had full court.

"Benny was the police's number one suspect in Ed North's disappearance," Doña Amada said with a smirk. "I hear he still is."

Chapter Two

DANA WENT HOME, her head swirling with the new unpleasant information Doña Amada was too glad to share with her.

It was almost six thirty p.m. When she first got home, she fired up Google and went down the rabbit hole that was the life and disappearance of Ed North. Sprinkled in the news articles about Ed North's disappearance was Benny's name. It was surreal to read about it.

After about ninety minutes down that rabbit hole, Dana had enough. She poured herself a glass of wine, a Cabernet from one of her favorite wineries from back home in Northern California, Pride Mountain Vineyards, which sat on top of Spring Mountain in Napa Valley wine country.

Dana grabbed her e-reader and headed upstairs to her veranda with Wally, the cat, leading the way. Wally bounced up the stairs, trying to beat her to their favorite lounge chair.

Dana plopped down on the chair, jockeying for a spot with Wally. She found the sweet spot and curled up with the kitty, the e-reader, and a glass of wine. She took a sip and smiled at the good grapes. Although she desperately wanted to, she couldn't stop thinking about Ed North and Benny. He was stopping by later and she had so many questions, but for now, all she could do was wait. At least she was sitting on her favorite lounge chair in her favorite spot of the house. Dana's home's nickname was Casa Verde—Green House in Spanish—because it was nestled between the thick tropical forest that borders Mariposa Beach and the gorgeous turquoise waters of the northern Pacific Coast.

It got dark pretty fast in Costa Rica—by six p.m. it was dead dark, year-round. Costa Rica didn't have faux time changes like in the United States. So she sat in the dark, the only light coming from a lamp with a soft blue light to mitigate attracting flying insects and the hue of the e-reader as she read the latest crime thriller by Lisa Regan. She could hear a chorus of crickets and cicadas in full force, along with a few guttural grunts of the howler monkeys that joined the chorus. Dana knew that Elvis, the nickname she had given to the loudest howler monkey that lived up in the trees just over on the other side of her property wall, wouldn't kick up his howling until around three in the morning.

There were floating lights off in the distance, courtesy of fireflies and the luminescent click beetles that lived up in the mountains. It was truly a magical spot that reminded Dana of an enchanted Fairy forest.

The afternoon showers cooled things for the evening, dropping the humidity level down into the comfort zone. Wally, the white cat of an unknown breed that had adopted her when she first moved in, was curled up next to her, purring like a buzz saw. It was Dana's favorite time of the year. She would read a few pages and look up, watching for the lights of Benny's truck coming up her long driveway, but it was pitch-black out there.

Dana and Benny didn't live together. He only lived part time in Mariposa Beach. The rest of the time, he was in Escazú, which was a suburb of the Costa Rican capital of San José, one hundred fifty miles away. It was a long drive on a two-lane highway jam-packed with semitrucks, buses, and cars that snaked down from the northeastern slopes of the Escazú Mountains to the coastal area of Nicoya, where Mariposa Beach was located. On a good day, it was about a four-hour drive.

Benny's family had long owned a beach house in Mariposa Beach, so he spent a lot of time there, and now that Dana and Benny were a couple, he spent even more time in Mariposa Beach. He could work from there unless he had court dealings or closings in the capital, so he spent more and more of his time in Mariposa Beach. Dana suspected that if it weren't for Benny's ten-year-old daughter, he might have made the move to Mariposa Beach a permanent one.

Dana checked the time on her phone. Benny would stop by soon. She wondered if he knew about the podcast. Dana hadn't mentioned it to him when they talked briefly over the phone. She wanted to ask him about it right away, since she couldn't help feeling a little hurt that he had never told her about Ed North. They spent many times talking about their past lives as they got to know each other. *It's just odd*, Dana thought. Having a client go missing and then being a suspect in Ed's disappearance seemed like something he should have mentioned to her—especially after her own entanglements with the police when they suspected her of murdering her cousin, with whom she was involved in a legal dispute over her inheriting Casa Verde. It would have been nice for Benny to say, *I know what you're going through.* But he hadn't. Hadn't mentioned it once in the year they had known each other.

Perhaps he was embarrassed and just didn't want to think about that period of his life anymore. Lord knows she didn't like thinking about the mess that had gone down with her murdered cousin.

Dana had tried to get more information about the whole enchilada of what had gone on with Ed North and Benny from

Doña Amada, but the old lady was satisfied just lighting the match and running off with her coffee and muffin order, a my-work-here-is-done smirk on her wrinkly face.

Dana then turned to Mindy and Leo for the details, but Mindy put the kibosh on her husband's loose lips on the matter.

"Honey, you need to talk to Benny about it. It's not right for us to gossip behind his back."

Dagnabbit. Dana hated when Mindy was right like that about such things.

Benny arrived at Casa Verde at seven. He had stopped at his home, which was across town from where Dana lived. But in tiny Mariposa Beach, that was a less than ten-minute drive. He unpacked, took a quick shower to wash away the stress of the treacherous four-hour drive down the twists and turns of the Pan-American Highway. Many Tico drivers took to it as if it were the pristine and speed-limit–free German Autobahn, which it was not. By a long shot.

Dana saw the headlights of his SUV bouncing up and down the gravel driveway.

Their relationship was now at a juncture where he had the code to the front gate, and it was no longer necessary for him to ring the front gate buzzer to be let inside.

As confused as she felt about Benny not sharing what he had gone through with Ed North, those ugly feelings dissipated when she saw the headlights getting closer as she heard the crunching gravel from her driveway getting louder. She smiled, sipping from her glass of wine. She hadn't seen Benny in three days, so she was just happy to see him. The Ed North business could wait a little longer for now.

She stood up and leaned over the veranda, looking down like a Southern belle as Benny exited the car.

"Hello there," she said, almost demurely holding up her glass of wine.

Benny looked up with his floppy brown hair and black eyes and a big smile taking over his brown face. "You started without me."

"I have a glass waiting for you. Come on up."

He went into the house and up the stairs and through her bedroom, out to the patio doors leading to the veranda. She smiled, hearing him making his way posthaste. It sounded like he took the stairs two at a time.

The patio door slid open and Benny stepped out.

"Well, hello there, gorgeous."

"I hope you're talking to me and not the glass of wine," Dana said, smiling. They hugged and kissed, and she offered him a glass of red wine. He glanced down at the bottle of Pride wine.

"Wow, the good stuff. What's the occasion?" Benny asked. He swirled the wine in his glass a few times, then brought the glass up to his nose and took a breath, smiling at the pleasing aroma of the grapes. And took a sip.

"There shouldn't be a need for a special occasion to enjoy the good stuff, don't you think?"

"I agree. Cheers." They clinked their glasses together and took a sip of wine. Dana didn't want to ruin the moment, so she would wait before bringing up the name of Benny's missing client.

Chapter Three

WITH THE BOTTLE of wine empty, Dana and Benny eventually made their way downstairs to the couch as they turned on the television and fired up the Netflix app.

Wally appeared out of nowhere and jumped onto the couch, circling a few times before plopping between Dana and Benny. The kitty snuggled up to Dana and gave Benny a smug look.

"Your darn cat still hates me."

"It's a love triangle type of thing," Dana said, smiling as she petted Wally.

Benny laughed as he picked up the remote control.

"What are you in the mood for?" he asked as he began scrolling through the array of choices between movies, television shows, and documentaries that made choosing something to watch feel overwhelming.

"Actually, I've been wanting to ask you about something," Dana said. She felt the guilt tongs tossing her insides like a salad. But with a failed marriage behind her, she swore to herself to always be honest with the people in her life. Keeping secrets or tiptoeing through difficult topics festered into anxiety and turned into communication breakdown, which was a relationship killer.

"Sure, what's up?" Benny asked, sounding curious.

"I was listening to one of my favorite true crime podcasts and the host announced that for her next series she was looking into the case of a man that went missing here in Costa Rica. Some rich guy named Ed North."

Dana could see him tense up after she mentioned Ed North's name. His facial expression turned from curious amusement to one of anxious trepidation. He put down the remote control and sighed.

"I was hoping they would drop this idea of making what happened to Ed into their next circus show."

"You knew about it?" Dana felt hurt. What other secrets was he keeping from her?

When Dana moved to Mariposa Beach from San Francisco, she was adamant about her disdain for secrets in a relationship. It was something her ex-husband was very good at, and when all those secrets came out during their split, she vowed *never again*. And she had been crystal clear about that when she and Benny moved their relationship from friends to couplehood.

And now his secrets were coming out. But she kept her hurt and anger in check. She wanted to hear him out. After all, it's not as if they were married, and maybe her no-secret mantra was just an unachievable fantasy in a relationship.

"The host of this podcast... What's her name?" Benny said, trying to pull the name from memory.

"Cheyenne Lively," Dana answered for him.

"Yes, that's it, Cheyenne Lively. She contacted me a few months ago. One of her producers too. They said they were looking into Ed's case for their true crime podcast, so they wanted to interview me. I told them I was not interested and had no comment. They kept pestering me nonstop, so I sent them a one-page statement giving them the general facts about my involvement with Ed North, and that I had no comment about his disappearance and no interest in participating in their podcast. That I had no more comments to make and asked them to not contact me again. Then I blocked them on my phone, email, and on Facebook just in case they kept trying to bug me."

"Why didn't you tell me about all this?"

"We had just started dating when they first contacted me, so I wasn't comfortable telling you about it. The way I saw it, there really wasn't much to tell. Ed was my client. He went missing. I don't know what happened to him. I shut down the podcast people and blocked them. And just moved on. It's not a part of my life that I like to relive. Especially with the likes of Cheyenne Lively."

"But we watch all those true crime shows on TV and I'm always listening to a true crime podcast. You didn't think it would be of note to share that one of the podcasts I listen to had reached out to you? That they want to do a show about a case that involves you?"

"I didn't know you were listening to Cheyenne Lively's podcast."

"She was one of the most popular true crime podcasters. Each episode gets millions of downloads," Dana said, sounding incredulous.

"I didn't know that. I didn't know you liked her and listened to her podcast, nor that she was that popular, which makes this whole circus that's about to hit town even worse. Dredging up things from my past, from seven years ago; things that I want to leave behind me forever. Now, for this podcaster to get her millions of downloads and her lucrative sponsorship deals, my name will once again be dragged through the mud so she can make her big bucks."

Benny's face looked ashen. Dana had gone from feeling

anger toward him to feeling bad. All those podcast and true crime shows she watched comfortably removed from the reality that real people were involved. Some, like family members, welcomed the attention of trying to find justice and bring closure, but others, like Benny, were collateral damage. Their wish for privacy and just being left alone would be ignored, all to produce a show that would entertain true crime junkies like herself. She could hear Cheyenne Lively's smooth made-for-radio voice reverberating in her head, calling her fans... calling her... *my true crime fiends*. Before that moment, she thought it was silly fun. Now she actually felt like a fiend.

"So what exactly happened, Benny?"

Benny took a deep breath.

"I'm not lying to you. I really don't know. Ed North was one of my first American clients. I was only two years out of law school. My first rich client. So I was excited. He was a nice guy. A bit odd. Somewhat demanding at times. But many clients are. I have had far worse since then. He was a New Yorker. Grew up poor in the Bronx and had that tough New York City edge to him. By the time I met him, he had moved to Florida. He had just married his second wife. She was about thirty years younger than Ed. I liked him. But I did not like his wife. Terri. She was a real piece of work."

"In what way?"

"You know me. I try not to judge people and keep an open mind, but she tested my mantra. She had been married to Ed, who was fifty-five then, for a couple of years. She had worked various jobs before then. Waitress. Barista. Hair stylist. Yoga instructor. Psychic. Now that she married a rich businessman, she fancied herself a Jackie O type of sophisticated woman, but she was just a few years removed from her trailer-park days. I have nothing against trailer parks, but I can't stand people putting on airs. And she was an expert at that. It probably didn't help that we were so close age-wise."

"I googled her, and she seems to be the number-one suspect in her husband's disappearance," Dana said.

"My money would be on her being the guilty party if I had to put down a wager on it."

"Did you have to deal a lot with her?"

"Luckily, no. She didn't care much for Costa Rica, especially down here on the coast. She was more of a South Beach, Florida, type, so she stayed away."

"You might have been reflecting your opinion about his wife on him," Dana said with a grin. "So he bought land here?"

"Yes. He bought a large plot of land about ten miles from Mariposa Beach, up in the mountains. It was an old coffee farm. About six acres, if I recall. It was a beautiful property over the Buena Vista River, with amazing views of the tropical forest, and it overlooked the Pacific Ocean. Ed loved that land. He wanted to move there permanently and set up an animal refuge. But Terri would have none of that. She complained about the humidity, even though she was born and raised in South Florida. The unpaved roads. The remoteness of it all. And she wasn't keen on animals, so the idea of having an animal refuge didn't sit well with her either."

"That must have caused a lot of friction in the marriage," Dana said.

"Sure felt that way. But can't totally blame her, though. She marries this rich guy. They live in Key Biscayne. They're members of the Miami Beach Golf Club. She shops at Bal Harbour. She's in her mid-twenties, living a stone's throw from South Beach, and that's the world she wanted to live in—not moving into an isolated old coffee farm in the middle of nowhere, Costa Rica, with her fifty-five-year-old husband."

"So him going missing solved those problems for her," Dana said.

"Indeed."

"And he left everything to her?"

"According to her, yes. But not to Ed's kids from his first marriage. Ed's other family has been the hair in Terri's soup for years. There was an official will, which was drafted by Ed's Florida attorney, not me. Almost everything was left to his three children. His first wife got the house they shared in Connecticut and some cash, but the kids got the bulk of the estate. However, after he went missing, Terri claims to have found a new will in which he left everything to her. In that new will, Ed supposedly cut off his kids and ex-wife from his estate. Something I find hard to believe he would do, but I guess you never know what is in someone's heart. But Ed's first wife and his kids don't believe it and they've been fighting over the estate for years. I stopped keeping tabs on it a few years ago, but I wouldn't be surprised if the legal fighting between Ed's kids, wife number one, and wife number two was still going on. A lot of bitterness to keep lawyers on both sides fat and happy."

"What a mess."

"That it was. After Ed's disappearance, his wife Terri told the police that he was heading down here. She said he was meeting me here about some big secret deal, but that wasn't true. I wasn't expecting him. Somewhere between Miami and Costa Rica, he vanished. He hasn't been seen or heard from since. Terri didn't even report him missing until his kids started asking where he was. It was only then that Terri filed a missing persons report. She said he was coming to spend a month down here, which is why she hadn't been worried, since he'd been gone for only three weeks at the time that she filed the report."

"Did she talk to him during that time?"

"She told the police in Florida, Costa Rica, and the American Embassy in San José that the landline was down at the farm and his cell phone service didn't work in the area. I checked. The landline was fine. And the cell phone reception, although spotty, it worked. She deflected on that and said that Ed had told her he was working on a deal with some shady people, but didn't give her the details. Then Terri threw me under the bus by telling the police that I had made the arrangements with these shady characters for this supposed business deal. So the OIJ was all over me, and Terri was way too eager to let me twist in the wind with her insinuations and innuendos that I might know what happened to her husband. Or that I knew the people responsible for his disappearance. I thought my legal practice was over. Who's going to hire a lawyer suspected of killing one of his clients?"

Dana took Benny's hand in her hands and caressed it.

"They never found his body or proof that he was even dead or any evidence of malfeasance from me or Terri or anyone, so the case went cold. Last I heard about Terri was on the fifth year of Ed's disappearance, which is when under Florida statutes she could legally declare him as presumed dead. Terri filed on the day of the fifth-year anniversary of Ed's disappearance and inherited his estate."

Chapter Four

THE NEXT DAY, Dana was at her bookstore slash cafe. She was filling in Mindy about her talk with Benny last night.

"I was mad at him at first for not telling me about this part of his past, but honestly, now I just feel terrible for him. You know how fast and loose the gossip flies around the beach towns," Dana said.

"Do I ever," Mindy said. "So what's he going to do?"

"For one, he's going to stop ignoring the oncoming onslaught of interest, so he unblocked Cheyenne Lively. He agreed to meet her when she arrives in town."

"When is that?"

"Tomorrow."

"Wow, she's not wasting time."

"I suppose this has been on the planning stages for months, and now it's all coming to a head since the first episode of the podcast is scheduled to drop next month."

"How are you doing with all this, honey?" Mindy asked.

"I'm fine. I was mad at Benny for not sharing any of this with me, but I get it. It's part of his life he hoped was long gone and forgotten. I'm actually helping him figure how to handle the media attention the podcast might kick off for him," Dana said.

Before trading her big-city life in San Francisco for small-town living in Mariposa Beach, Dana worked in public relations. She had majored in Media Studies at Berkeley, then graduated from the UC Berkeley Graduate School of Journalism. She spent the first half of her working life as a print journalist, a career going the way of the Dodo bird. After years of salary cuts, freezes, and downsizing in print journalism, she switched careers. She went to the dark side, as she called it, into public relations. It was mostly unfulfilling work for her, but the job security and nice salary that actually increased every year was a delightful change of pace. But she had left all that behind when she moved to Mariposa Beach. She was now living the beach life as a permanent tourist, running her little bookstore, and she loved it. But she also loved Benny, so for him, she was more than willing to put back on her PR hat to make sure Cheyenne Lively and the juggernaut podcast network she worked for wouldn't gobble up Benny in their quest for publishing another über-popular and lucrative true crime podcast with him caught in the middle of it.

A few miles away, just as Dana was working on the media strategy for Benny, Ed North's wife, Terri, was checking into the Tranquil Bay Luxury Resort near Mariposa Beach. She had remarried, so now went by the name of Terri Kaminski. Husband number two, Burt Kaminski, was standing next to her. They made quite the odd couple. Terri was short and stocky, with long, flowing blonde hair and sparkling green eyes. Burt was tall and thin, like a flagpole.

Burt was admiring the lobby of the five-star resort with its sweeping views of the Pacific Ocean. His ogling annoyed Terri.

"Get a move on it, Burt. I want to make my stay in this Podunk country as brief as possible," she seethed.

"I don't know, dear, it's nice down here. Pretty swanky hotel," Burt said.

"It's a resort, not a hotel, and yeah, this place is nice, but the rest of this town is the pits. Small, hot, full of bugs that will make your skin crawl, and there's nothing to do here but bake in the sun or get eaten by mosquitoes," Terri said loudly enough for everyone in the lobby to hear it, including the local staff. The front desk clerk had to bear and grin at the rude blabbermouth standing in front of her.

"Checking in?" the clerk asked. She was petite and pretty. Brown skin, long, raven-black hair, and stunning topaz-colored eyes. The name Becky Morales was etched into her name tag.

"You're a smart cookie, aren't 'cha?" Terri said with venomous rudeness and condescension.

"Honey," Burt said, as if trying to reel in his wife's awful behavior.

"Oh, put a sock on it, Burt. Let's just get this over with."

Becky finished checking them in. She handed over the room card keys and directed them toward the bell hop who would take them and their luggage up to their room. Terri turned away to follow the bell hop before turning back to Becky.

"Say, how far is Mariposa Beach from here?"

"It's very close, Mrs. Kaminski. It's a beautiful ten-minute walk down the Emerald pathway, which leads you from the resort right into Mariposa Beach. Or our concierge would be happy to make other transportation arrangements for you. We have a shuttle that goes down to town often, or you can hire a private car."

"Good. Do you know where the Bagels, Books, and Lattes coffee shop is located?" Terri asked.

"Oh, yes, everyone knows where that is. You'll find good books there, and Mindy's bagels are..."

"I didn't ask for a Yelp review. Is. It. Far. From. Here?"

Becky swallowed hard. "No, ma'am, it's right on Main Street in Mariposa Beach. If you take the pathway down from the resort, you'll run right into the cafe in about fifteen minutes."

"Excellent," Terri said, turning away from Becky and walking away toward the bellhop without even bothering to thank the young clerk.

As soon as the Kaminskis were gone, the entire front lobby staff seemed to breathe a collective sigh of relief.

"Whoa, who the heck are they?" Becky asked.

Becky's shift leader, Mauricio Sánchez, filled her in.

"That's the crazy lady that killed her rich husband like ten years ago."

"Really?" Becky said.

"Well, it's never been proven, which is why she's free with his money, I suppose."

"Her husband's body was never found," one bellhop added in.

"How do you guys know about all this?"

"Well, you were too young back then, but it was big news around here when her husband vanished. And they have covered the story on Dateline and 20/20," Mauricio said.

"Not only that. There was also a show about the case on the Oxygen Network. And now there is a podcaster doing a big investigation about it. My cousin said the podcaster is airbnb-ing a house in Mariposa Beach," the bellhop added.

"So, are they going to be part of the show?" Becky wondered.

"Doubtful. She's probably going to try stopping the show," Mauricio said ominously.

Becky looked around with concern. "I better warn my friend that works at Bagels, Books, and Lattes that this nutjob was asking for directions there," Becky said, picking up her cell phone.

Chapter Five

Amalfi Soto worked at Bagels, Books, and Lattes. Dana had hired her to work the register on the bookstore side of the bookstore slash cafe. But since Mindy's coffee shop was always a lot busier than the bookstore, Amalfi also ran the register for Mindy and even had become a topnotch barista. Before working for Dana and Mindy, she had worked at the Tranquil Bay Resort—a job she disliked, since it was run with a tight iron fist by the resort's owner, Gustavo Barca. Barca had an open offer to buy Dana's property, which she kept turning down. The rich developer and hotelier even tried to play hardball with her by bankrolling a bogus lawsuit to take the property away from her. She had prevailed, thanks in part to Benny's legal work, but it had been a stressful experience in her life, so she still couldn't find it in herself to forgive Gustavo Barca for what he'd put her through—not that he'd ever asked for forgiveness. For him, it had been just a business play. For Dana, it had been her new home and life at play. So she took a modicum of delight to have hired Amalfi Soto away from Gustavo's resort, which was the primary employer in town.

Becky Morales called Amalfi. They chatted for a few

minutes. After hanging up with Becky, Amalfi turned to Dana, who was writing a press release for Benny on her laptop—a press release she hoped she wouldn't have to send out.

"Dana, I just got off the phone with my friend Becky, who works at the resort," Amalfi said trepidatiously.

Dana looked up from her laptop.

"Do you know who Terri Kaminski is?"

Dana recognized the name. She had gone down deep into the rabbit hole that was Ed North's life and case. She knew well that Terri North had remarried and went by Terri Kaminski now.

"I do. Why are you asking about her?"

Amalfi told Dana what Becky had said about her unpleasant encounter with Terri at the resort.

"Terri Kaminski is in the country right now?"

Amalfi nodded. "She just checked in at the resort with her husband twenty minutes ago."

"Oh, brother, she must have gotten word about the podcaster coming to town to work on the Ed North story," Dana said.

"That's not good," Leo added, having overheard the conversation.

"That lady asked Becky how to get to the bookstore cafe," Amalfi said.

Dana thought about it for a moment as Amalfi and Mindy looked worried.

"Mindy's food and coffee are well known on the Nicoya Peninsula. It's in all the travel books and the hotels all recommend it, so maybe it's just that," Dana said. She hoped that was the case, but deep down inside, she knew that was just wishful thinking.

Dana went into her office at the back of the bookstore slash cafe so she could close the door and have some privacy to call Benny, who was working from home. He picked up her call right away.

"Are you busy? Do you have a moment?"

He said he could talk, so she told him about Terri being in town.

"She's here? At the resort?" Benny said, not believing it.

"As we speak. According to Amalfi's friend working at the resort."

"Well, that's a kicker."

"What do you think she's doing here, Benny?"

"She's not here on a vacation, I can guarantee you that."

"Are you sure about that?"

"Oh, yeah. The way she feels about Costa Rica and everything that has gone down with Ed and the cloud of suspicion over her head as being Ed's killer, this is the last place she would want to be."

"So why is she here then?"

Benny sighed. "I'm sure we're going to find out soon enough, but I suspect she's here to stop the podcast from featuring Ed North's case."

"She can't do that. Can she?"

"She has all of Ed's money, which means she can afford a small army of pit bull lawyers to be at her beck and call. Those lawyers are aggressively litigious. Bullying people into silence is their bread and butter. If anyone can kill a story like this from seeing the light of day, it's Terri and her legal goons," Benny explained.

"What do we do now?" Dana asked.

"I'm going to call Cheyenne back. Let's stay put until I talk to her."

"Sounds good," Dana said as she glanced at the computer monitor on her desk, where the store's four security cameras displayed in a gallery view the comings and goings of the bookstore slash cafe. She had one camera covering the front parking lot area, one at the back, and two inside. Dana leaned in to watch a familiar face walk into her bookstore slash cafe as she talked to Benny on the phone.

"Holy Toledo, you will not believe this," Dana said.

"What is it?" Benny asked.

"I glanced at one of my security cameras just as a customer with a familiar face walked in."

"Oh crud, is it Terri?" Benny asked.

"Nope. Cheyenne Lively, the podcaster of the hour, just walked into the store."

Cheyenne Lively walked inside the Books, Bagels, and Lattes shop. She looked to her left and saw the small but decently stocked bookstore. A young girl sat behind the register, smiling at her. There weren't any customers, so the youngster seemed excited at the prospect of a customer. Cheyenne smiled back for a moment, then she turned to the other side of the building where she could see the cafe.

"May I help you find something?" Amalfi asked.

"I'm looking for Dana Kirkpatrick. Is she available?" Cheyenne asked.

"Um..." Amalfi wasn't sure how to respond.

"It's okay, Amalfi. Ms. Lively, please join me inside my office," Dana said, standing under the doorframe of her office.

Cheyenne flashed a smile at Amalfi and at Mindy and Leo, who were gawking at her.

Dana watched as Cheyenne made her way toward her. A confident gait. Dana knew her bio by heart. She was thirty years old. Born and raised in Columbus, Nebraska. She made it into the collegiate big leagues when she attended Columbia University in New York City. She went to the Columbia Journalism School, which was one of the oldest journalism schools in the world and the only journalism school in the Ivy League. That was some serious collegiate achievement. When Dana was applying to colleges to study journalism, she had applied to Columbia, but had not made the cut, and she wasn't a slouch in the academic achievement department.

After graduating, Cheyenne worked as a journalist in New York and Los Angeles, but after just a few years she switched gears, becoming a researcher, writer, and producer for television network news programs like Dateline and 20/20, where she made her bones in true crime infotainment before becoming a full-time true crime podcaster two years ago.

Cheyenne walked right up to Dana with a big smile, holding out her right hand to Dana.

"It's a pleasure to meet you, Dana," Cheyenne said.

Dana shook her hand. Firm. They looked each other in the eye. Both strong, independent women. Journalists by training, now doing very different work. Although Dana couldn't help but feel a tinge of jealously. And for the first time, she felt a little embarrassed about her career choices. She owned a small, fledgling bookstore in a tiny beach-town community in Costa Rica while Cheyenne was the host of one of the biggest podcasts out there with millions of downloads, which meant she was raking in some big-time money for her work and living the jet-set life in L.A.

"Likewise. I'm a fan of your podcast," Dana said. She felt

her cheeks redden.

"Thank you. May I come in?"

Dana realized she was still standing in the doorframe, basically blocking the entrance to her office. She quickly stepped backward.

"Of course, sorry, please come in."

Cheyenne looked around the small office, which made Dana feel insecure again.

"Can I get you a coffee or tea? Mindy's coffee is the best."

"I've heard that it is, but not right now, thank you," Cheyenne said, sitting down on the guest chair across from Dana's desk. Dana went around her desk and sat.

"Thank you so much for agreeing to meet with me," Cheyenne said as she riffled through a black backpack. She pulled out a portable recorder.

"Do you mind if I record this?"

You don't waste time, Dana thought. Her feelings of insecurity and embarrassment dissipated at seeing the recorder. She agreed to meet with Cheyenne not because she was one of her true crime fiends, but to ensure an Ivy Leaguer did not railroad Benny.

"No, for now I'll only talk with you off the record. If that's a problem, then—"

Cheyenne interrupted her. "Not a problem at all. Off the record," she said, putting the recorder back in her backpack. "Believe it or not, I'm here for the truth. For justice and to help Benny," Cheyenne said with a big smile.

Cheyenne Lively was pretty, with fair skin tones that would be a challenge to protect in the tropics. Dana figured she would need to lather up with SPF 50+++ while in Mariposa Beach.

She had shoulder-length light reddish hair the color of a faded strawberry pulled back into a ponytail.

Confidence oozed from her, and she had a dogged, no-

nonsense look, which was probably why she was so successful as an investigative journalist and true crime podcaster.

"Who said Benny needs help? Help from what?"

"Well, you've heard the innuendo and what Terri North Kaminski says happened to her husband and Benny's role in it?"

"Not really. What does Terri say happened to her husband?" Dana was half-playing dumb. All she knew so far about this sordid affair was what she had researched on the internet and what Benny had told her last night.

"That he came to Costa Rica for a business deal put together by Benny. That deal went south and Mr. North was murdered. And that Benny was involved, or at the very least he helped get rid of the body, ensuring they would never find it."

Dana was taken aback by Cheyenne's recollection of events. It was unsettling to even suggest that Benny would be capable of something so horrible.

"You're telling me that there are rumors that Benny got away with murder?" Dana said.

"Yes. I'm sorry. I know you're in relationship with Mr. Campos."

Dana's eyebrows furrowed. Cheyenne was showing off the investigative in investigative journalism.

"There is no need to apologize. Rest assured Benny was not involved in any of these shenanigans with Mr. North."

"Then help me with my investigation. Let me help you finally clear his name, for good," Cheyenne said.

Dana's eyebrows furrowed again, and she felt self-conscious about her brow dancing around nervously.

It was an intriguing proposition. But deep down, she wondered if she could really trust the podcaster. Dana remembered her days as a journalist. She recognized that look of a journalist on a story like a dog on a meaty new bone, and Dana feared Benny was Cheyenne's meaty bone.

Chapter Six

DANA WASN'T ABOUT to commit to anything, so after their talk Dana walked Cheyenne out of her office into the bookstore slash cafe as Amalfi, Mindy, and Leo looked on like drivers rubbernecking at a wreck on the side of the road.

Dana agreed to talk to Benny about all this and to decide whether he would agree to talk to her—on the record. Dana liked Cheyenne, but she figured that was a common reaction to meeting such a charismatic and polished person. Liking was a far cry from trusting. At that moment, Dana felt like she couldn't trust the podcaster as far as she could throw her.

Just as they reached the front door leading out to Main Street, in walked Terri and Burt Kaminski.

The four of them stood there looking at each other oddly. Dana couldn't help but notice that Terri had continued to marry older; Burt had a good fifteen years on her. She stood there with her big, blonde hair. She had red rouge on her cheeks and a bright red lipstick. Burt had salt-and-pepper hair cut short and combed to the right—cowlick style. He wore lightweight titanium eyeglasses with thin arms. He looked like he was there to sell them insurance.

The four of them stood face-to-face for a moment. They exchanged awkward glances at each other for just a second or two as Terri's eyes widened and her face flushed over her rouge in recognition of what she was seeing.

Dana stood next to Cheyenne. She might have as well waved a red cape in front of a furious snorting bull, shouting *olé*.

"I knew you two were up to no good!" Terri seethed.

Before Dana or Cheyenne could react or say anything, Terri went off screaming like a boiling teakettle.

"What conniving scheme are you two little tomatoes working on to help that murdering dog, Benny? Scheming how to pin my poor Ed's murder on me, are you?"

Dana tried to speak but couldn't get a word in.

"Well, I'm not letting you get away with it. My life will not be fodder for you stupid little podcast, missy," Terri hissed at Cheyenne, then turned her venom toward Dana.

"And you. Shame on you. Helping your murderer of a boyfriend cover up his crime and teaming up with this one here on that stupid podcast. How much is she paying you?"

It was time for Dana's teakettle to scream.

"How dare you come into my place of business shooting your mouth off with absurd claims? If anyone is covering for a murderer, it's *you*, covering for killing your first husband."

Terri looked over at Burt as if to say, *You're going to let her talk to me like this?* But he just stood there, watching the spectacle.

"Please, ladies, this accomplishes nothing," Cheyenne said.

Terri wasn't having any of it. She reached into her purse. For a moment Dana flinched, worried she going to whip out a gun, but she came up holding a folder.

"This all ends right now. Here is an injunction from you doing your stupid little show on my Ed. And here are NDAs for everyone here to sign," Terri barked, looking around the bookstore slash cafe.

Dana was glad that at least it was near closing time during the slow tourist season, so there weren't any customers watching the fireworks flying, recording it all to go viral on Twitter.

"I'm not signing a darn thing," Dana said.

"Ditto," Mindy said, standing with her arms crossed, glaring at Terri.

"Mrs. Kaminski, as I've told you dozens of times, since you refuse to talk to me on the record about your husband's case and you keep threatening me with lawsuits and sending me and my network one cease-and-desist letter after another, I'm not talking with you about anything else anymore, and I'm sure as heck not signing anything without the advice of my network's lawyers. If you change your mind and want to talk to me, calmly and on the record, to state your case and air your concerns, then please call me," Cheyenne said cool as a cucumber, proffering her business card to Terri.

Terri took the card, and without looking at it she tore it in two and tossed the torn-up pieces into the air.

"That's enough," Leo Salas thundered. "You two, out. This is private property. Out now. Or I'll call the police."

Terri stood there for a moment, fuming.

"If you don't leave in ten seconds, I'm calling the police," Dana said, whipping out her cell phone.

"This is far from over. You two will regret tangling with me and getting into my personal affairs," Terri said, spinning around so aggressively that she almost tripped. "Let's go, Burt," she screeched as she stormed out. Burt gave everyone a quick glance before following his wife out the door. He didn't say a word during the whole confrontation.

"That went well," Cheyenne said with a grin.

"Holy moly, she's a piece of work," Dana said.

"She's a handful, that's for sure," Cheyenne said.

"You must be used to dealing with upset people like that a lot in your line of work," Leo said.

"Part of the job. But don't worry about her. She's a hot mess. And whatever you do, don't sign anything she gives you. Get a lawyer if she keeps pushing to sign these NDAs or whatever she's pushing for us to sign," Cheyenne said.

Cheyenne looked at Dana and handed her a business card. "Call me as soon as you talk with Benny about what we talked."

Dana just nodded, looking at the business card in her hands.

"Goodbye, everyone. I will be back for your homemade bagels and cream cheese. I've heard it's the bomb," Cheyenne said, walking outside.

Mindy walked over to Dana and put her arm around her.

"You okay, honey?"

Dana laughed. "I'm fine. You know me, I'm like honey near a beehive, always attracting these buzzing angry bees into my life."

Chapter Seven

DANA LEFT her bookstore and drove straight to Benny's house. Her head was still whizzing in an almost delirious state after the confrontation with Terri Kaminski. She kept seeing her Tammy Faye made-up face turning beet red in anger, her nostrils flaring as she accused Benny of murder.

It was probably a good thing Benny wasn't there. It would have been like tossing kerosene into an already raging fire had Terri seen Benny and Cheyenne together.

Benny had been working from home and he had been too busy to break away, having had several calls with clients scheduled throughout the day.

Back in the city, he rented office space in Escazú. It was a small commercial building centrally located in the biggest expat community of Costa Rica, with easy highway access to the airport and the beaches on both coasts—the Pacific and the Atlantic. There were six offices in total which were occupied by two other lawyers, an accountant, a marketing and SEO consultant, and an importer-exporter of essential oils. All the tenants shared a conference room, break area, and a front desk receptionist. It was a great setup for Benny that allowed him to keep his overhead costs down. However, since meeting Dana he was spending more and more time in Mariposa Beach working out of a guest bedroom he had converted into an office. He could make his client calls easily enough, but the internet connection in Mariposa Beach was only fine for personal use; for work, the connection wasn't up to par with the lightning-fast connection he had in his Escazú office. Dana didn't want to be in the way of his business, but he insisted that the convenience of not having to make the long drive back and forth was worth it.

Dana had texted to let Benny know she was on her way and about running into Terri.

Oh boy, is all he texted back.

As most places in tiny Mariposa Beach, it was a quick drive from Dana's bookstore to Benny's house, which was located right on the outskirts of town. It took her six minutes to make the drive. A little slower than usual, since the rainy season chewed up the already pockmarked roads around town even more, forcing her to drive extra defensively as she zigzagged across the road to avoid a road washout and potholes the size of sink holes.

At least the afternoon rains had stopped by five o'clock. Dana kept the soft top on her cherry red Willys Jeep in place just in case an errant rain shower might decide to sneak up on her — a lesson she had learned the hard and wet way at the start of the rainy season.

Dana loved her 1940s fully restored Jeep. It was perfect for tooling around in coastal areas and through the mountains and forests that made up the Nicoya Peninsula.

Benny greeted her at the door with a kiss.

"You're a sight for sore eyes," he said.

"Aren't you sweet? Do you have more work calls?" Dana asked.

"All done, so I'm all ears about your big encounter with

Terri Kaminski. She's something, so I can only imagine the tale you have to tell."

Benny's house had been in his family for over fifty years. As rural as Mariposa Beach was now, back then it had been mostly jungle and the shoreline. The region had hardly been divided into the well-developed beach towns that now peppered the entire Guanacaste coast.

Benny was an only child, so when his parents passed he inherited the beach house, a house he had been visiting since he was a child.

They sat in his living room. Benny offered her something to drink. She went for the freshly made mango juice. She took a sip and sat down on the couch. He did the same. Dana filled Benny in with what had transpired over at the bookstore slash cafe with Terri. She told him about her ranting and raving, accusing them all of being up to no good, and about the NDAs she tried to bully them all into signing.

"Doesn't seem like she's changed a bit since the last time I had to deal with her craziness," Benny said.

Dana handed over the legal documents Terri had tossed on the counter before leaving.

"I'll look at these. It should be amusing," he said, opening the folder and taking a quick look at the documents.

"There was something else she was saying. Vile, awful stuff," Dana said sheepishly, looking down, embarrassed at bringing up Terri's wild accusations against him.

"About me, no doubt," Benny said calmly.

Dana nodded.

"Let me take a wild guess. I killed her husband. Got rid of the body. And how I've gotten away with murder all these years."

"That sums it up pretty well."

Benny sighed. "She's been barking up that tree for years. So it's not surprising she's still trying to pin Ed's disappearance on me."

"What do you think happened to Ed?" Dana asked.

"Between you and me, I think Terri killed him. They lived in a beautiful house on Biscayne Bay in Miami, with a boat and their own private dock. She grew up boating in Florida, so she knew her way around the waterways. She probably killed him and then tossed the body into Biscayne Bay, ensuring Ed's body would never be found."

"Why would she want to kill him?"

"During Ed's last trip to Costa Rica, he told me his marriage to Terri wasn't working out. He was talking to a divorce lawyer in Florida. Once all that was settled, he wanted to move down here permanently. He shared that with me so I could start getting the paperwork ready for that move. He was thinking it would take him about six months to sort through all that, then he would return to Costa Rica. The day after that conversation, he went back to the States, and that was the last time I ever saw or heard from him."

"Sure sounds like she had plenty of motive, but she's so tiny, and the photos I've seen of Ed North, he wasn't a small dude."

"Never underestimate short people. They're used to having to stick up for themselves, so they can be pretty tough. Terri had a rough childhood. Grew up dirt poor in a trailer park near the Everglades. She ran away from home at sixteen. Rumor has it—and this is only a rumor, but according to Ed's first wife, so take this with a grain of salt—she was hustling on the streets when she met Ed at age nineteen."

"What?"

"That's the rumor. Since she's keen on perpetrating the rumor that I killed Ed, I don't feel guilty telling you about the dark rumors surrounding her," Benny said.

"Did Ed tell you how they met?"

"Yes. I was out to dinner with Ed and Terri when I asked how they met. She got very skittish, and she began to nervously patter on about how she was hitchhiking and Ed gave her a ride. Then she quickly changed subjects, and that was the last of that topic. I could tell she didn't want to walk down memory lane."

"I guess I wouldn't, either."

"What did you think about Cheyenne Lively?" Benny asked.

"That's right. I've been so sidetracked with Terri showing up in town that I forgot to tell you about my meeting with Cheyenne."

"I can only imagine how seeing you two together set Terri off," Benny said with a sly grin.

"And how. I thought she might have a coronary."

"That would put this nightmare to rest."

"Benny!"

"I know, I know, that was mean. Too low. It's just that it drives me crazy. I was Ed's lawyer for all of ten months, and it's like the mess he left behind just won't go away from my life."

"I understand, honey," Dana said, taking his hand. She gave him a quick kiss.

"I digress. Tell me about Cheyenne. Can we trust her?" Benny asked.

"I wouldn't go that far. Her main motivator here is to produce another blockbuster true crime podcast, so you're fodder for that end goal. That said, she's bright and an amazing investigative reporter with Ivy League chops and plenty of experience investigating cases like these. Plus, she has the deep pockets of the DEQ Network."

"What's a DEQ Network?"

Dana laughed. "I forget you're not into podcasting like I am. The DEQ Podcasting Network is a top-five podcast publisher. They produce and publish dozens of shows every year with over one hundred million downloads per month. It's a big business. The network recently closed on a twenty-million-dollar round of funding."

Benny whistled. "You should get into podcasting," he said with a grin.

"Tell me about it. Anyway, the DEQ Network produces and publishes Cheyenne's podcast, so she has access to oodles of money to investigate this case. And she has an amazing knack for solving cold cases, just like this one, so if anyone can help us get to the truth about Ed's disappearance, it's Cheyenne Lively."

Chapter Eight

CHEYENNE LIVELY PULLED up to her Airbnb in her rented Suzuki Jimny off-road SUV.

The rental house was located three miles from Mariposa Beach. It was a cozy home cradled by the verdant mountains. It was a good location, close to Mariposa Beach and Ed North's old property, which was a few miles farther up the mountain. She was close to where she needed to be without being too close. She always kept where she was staying on the down-low, since her job usually ruffled more than a few feathers. And boy, had she ruffled Terri Kaminski's feathers.

She knew Terri was upset the moment she called her, three months ago, to tell the woman that she was making her first husband's mysterious disappearance the subject of the next podcast. Cheyenne always sought the participation of everyone involved in the shows she was working on, which meant reaching out to all the major players, from the victim's loved ones to the suspects to the police and lawyers that investigated the case, seeking justice. Usually, the people involved in the cases were eager to take part.

Cheyenne's show was in the top ten most downloaded

podcasts, which translated to millions of listeners and she had millions of social media followers, so people wanted to talk to her. Especially the victim's family, who were desperately seeking justice and to find out what happened to their loved ones. The cops and lawyers she had dealt with on her podcast were happy to be interviewed. It was a nice ego boost to be in such a popular podcast, plus they, too, wanted closure on cases they hadn't been able to solve.

It's why it was so strange to her that Terri refused to cooperate and tried to shut down the podcast with a bunch of legal motions. It was as if she didn't want to know what really happened to her first husband.

After working the true crime beat on network television and in podcasting, Cheyenne knew that usually those who were most upset over her showing up in their lives were those trying to hide something. So they usually made the top of her possible suspect list. And at the top of that list she had two people: Terri Kaminski and Benny Campos.

Although Terri was downright hostile toward her, Benny kept things more professional. She had been trying to get a hold of Benny Campos for months. He wasn't rude per se, but he had shut her down big time, blocking her in social media, email, and on his mobile phone.

After her encounter with Terri and being at the receiving end of her fury, Terri had floated up to the top of her suspect list.

The victim's family members usually were the ones welcoming her with open arms, thrilled that she was taking on the cold case of their loved ones on a popular podcast. Didn't Terri want to know what happened to Ed? Or perhaps she knew and wanted to make sure no one else would find out, especially a nosy podcaster.

Cheyenne walked into the house carrying her backpack,

which was jam-packed with her notes and podcasting equipment. She plopped down her backpack and purse with a loud sigh.

Nick Suárez walked out of one of the rooms in the back of the house.

"It went that well, huh?" Nick said.

Nick Suárez was one of the top podcast producers with the DEQ Podcast Network, and he spoke Spanish fluently, which would come in handy since Cheyenne's grasp of the language was spotty.

"An all-paid trip to Costa Rica? Heck, yeah, sign me up," he had told her excitedly when she had first asked him to be her producer on the project.

Nick was Mexican American from Orange County—an audio engineer with a decade of experience in sound for film, radio, television, and music. He'd joined DEQ three years ago to oversee the production of the network's podcasts. He had stayed back to set up their recording studio, and because Cheyenne didn't want to overwhelm Dana by showing up with her producer in tow.

"I need a drink," Cheyenne said, blowing a loose strand of red hair from her face.

"Coming right up," Nick said as he walked into the kitchen and took out two Imperial beers from the fridge. He removed the bottle caps, then handed a cold one to Cheyenne while he kept one for himself.

"Thanks," she said, taking a sip.

"So you met Dana, go on."

"The meeting with Dana Kirkpatrick wasn't too bad. She was standoffish, but nice. And she would only talk to me off the record."

"Ugh. 'Off the record'; I hate those three words," Nick said.

"Ditto. Anyway, toward the end, I think I got her to come

around to help us change Benny Campos's mind about talking to us, but she didn't commit, just said that she would talk to him."

"Better than shutting you down completely, so that doesn't sound too bad," Nick said.

"Fingers crossed. But like Billy Mays used to say, but wait, there's more," Cheyenne said, taking another sip of beer. "Then things really got kooky."

Nick looked at her with interest, his curiosity piqued. "Go on, you're killing me here."

"As I was leaving Dana's bookstore, I ran into Terri and Burt Kaminski, who showed up out of the blue."

"They're here in Costa Rica?" an incredulous Nick asked.

"In the flesh, and Terri is on the warpath. She cussed me out. She cussed Dana out. Heck, she even yelled at the other people who were there working with Dana."

"What did you say?"

"I tried to calm her down. I told her I still wanted to interview her, and I gave her my card, which she tore in half and threw back in my face."

"No way!"

"Oh yeah, my friend, then she tried to bully all of us at the bookstore into signing NDAs. As. If," Cheyenne said.

"Wow. Looks like I missed quite the show."

"So. How are things back here? You all set up?"

"Mr. DeMille is ready for your close up," Nick said with a grin.

"Let's check it out," Cheyenne said, walking to the room that Nick had selected to become their small recording studio.

Nick was methodical in the selection process of which room would make the best studio. They were renting a four-bedroom house. He used his bevy of gadgets to test the acoustics and whatnot. The sound-engineering stuff went over Cheyenne's head. That was Nick's job.

Once he picked the room, he went to work. The chosen location was a small room toward the back of the house. It was the maid's quarters, which had surprised Cheyenne, who assumed only mansions would have maid's rooms. Nick explained they were pretty common in most middle- and upper-class homes in Latin America, where manual labor was much cheaper than in the States, so they built many houses, not just mansions, with a room for a live-in maid. And for his audio purposes, the maid's room was the best spot in the house to use as the studio. So he went to work transforming it.

He took out the bed and dresser, but left the mattress, which would make a great sound absorber. He moved in a small conference table they had bought at an Office Depot near the airport in Alajuela. They had stocked up with the supplies they would need for the podcast. Nick then spent an hour working on the sound treatment covering the small bedroom's walls and ceiling with foam panels.

The room wasn't carpeted, which was a bummer from the sound perspective, but Nick was prepared for that, knowing that carpeting in the tropics would be as popular as air conditioning in Antarctica. He purchased a dozen cheap pillows from Walmart, which was conveniently located less than ten minutes from the Office Depot. Nick dropped the pillows around the mattress on the floor for further soundproofing. He then draped a sound-reduction mat that he had brought from the States on the conference table, set up the microphone stands on top of the mat, and three XLR microphones, each with its own filters to reduce popping sounds created in the pronunciation of plosives —an audio-quality killer for a podcast. Next to each mic, Nick laid down Sony headphones.

He had more microphones at the ready if Cheyenne needed

them, but he figured three would be just right, since he didn't think she would have to interview more than two people at once. He had also set up the computers they would use and his sound mixer.

Cheyenne walked into the new studio. She surveyed the room, liking what she saw. Her favorite microphone was ready for prime time. At the far end of the table was Nick's mixer, used to ensure the audio being recorded was amazing. On a second desk he had set up two 24" iMacs that they needed for the software to record and edit the podcast episodes, as well as to upload them to the DEQ server for final processing. The other computer she would use to write the scripts, show notes, and continue with the research process for the podcast.

"It looks amazing, Nick," Cheyenne said. She held her right hand in the air for a team-building high-five.

In another room, Cheyenne had set up her war room. She had two rolling white boards filled with her research and notes.

The other two rooms were Cheyenne's and Nick's bedrooms. She took the master bedroom, since she was the star of the podcast, as she had teased Nick, who rolled his eyes at her.

Cheyenne looked at her suspect board. Number one was Terri Kaminski. Number two, Benny Campos. Number three, she drew a question mark.

After a couple of hours of work, Cheyenne checked the time. It almost eight p.m. She was hungry. Living in Los Angeles, she was used to having food delivered with Uber Eats. She was delighted to learn that food delivery service was huge in Costa Rica, then crestfallen to find out that they were off the beaten path down on the coast, so she couldn't rely on the magical app to bring her food. She walked out of her war room and headed to the recording studio. Nick was on one of the computers.

"Hey Nick, what are we going to do about food?"

"Yeah, it just dawned on me that I stocked up on all the gear I needed for our studio but didn't get any food. Though I checked online and there are a couple of good restaurants in Mariposa Beach."

"Well, I'm starving, so let's go get a bite to eat and we'll hit the grocery store in the morning," Cheyenne said.

"Sounds like a plan."

Cheyenne and Nick made their way down to Mariposa Beach. Nick drove. Cheyenne texted Dana.

Heading to the Qué Vista Restaurant for dinner with my producer. Join us?

Cheyenne watched the phone for the three little dots to dance around on the screen, showing that Dana was writing a message back to her, but she didn't reply. Oh, well, she figured. She knew well that Dana didn't trust her, and she understood it. Cheyenne was used to it. She was, after all, in town to make a successful podcast.

Dana seemed nice enough to Cheyenne, but with or without her help, she was going to make another compelling and successful podcast series that her true crime fiends were going to love. She had to go where the case took her, even if that meant ticking people off—even people that she liked, like Dana. So, like it or not, Benny was going to be front and center in her podcast.

Chapter Nine

DANA LEFT Benny's place at nine p.m. He was due back in the city for a late-morning client meeting in his office in Escazú. He told Dana he felt talked-out about Cheyenne, Terri Kaminski, Ed North, and that dang podcast. She took that as her cue that it was time to go to her own place across town. Besides, Benny would be going to bed early so he could make the drive back to the city in the morning to try to beat the slow-as-molasses traffic.

Dana had seen and ignored Cheyenne's text message about inviting her to join Cheyenne and her producer for dinner. Her drive home through Main Street took her right by the Qué Vista Restaurant, making her think about the text message. Dana stopped at the turnoff from Main Street that led to the road up to Casa Verde. She sat in an idling Big Red for a moment, pondering if she should stop by the restaurant. Since the afternoon rain showers were done for the day, she had the top down. The evening had cooled nicely. She could hear the cacophony of creatures that came alive at night in the nearby forest, along with the gentle crashing of waves on the beach. Back home in bustling San Francisco, people played ambient noises through their apps or Alexa-type devices to help them relax in their concrete jungle. Here in Mariposa Beach, Dana had the real thing. She loved it. And she loved Benny. She couldn't ignore the pickle he was in, so if she could help Cheyenne, perhaps she could finally clear Benny's name with all this Ed North business. Dana put Big Red into first gear and turned left, away from Casa Verde and toward the restaurant.

It was late, so things were winding down at the restaurant. There were only a few people she could see as she pulled up. Dana spotted the small Suzuki Jimny SUV that she had seen Cheyenne climb into when she'd left the bookstore earlier that day, so she knew Cheyenne was still there. Dana felt a little nervous about her mini-stalking, but mostly about getting in cahoots with Cheyenne, someone she still couldn't trust. She knew Cheyenne was in it just for the podcast, not to help Benny clear his name. But perhaps those two things went hand in hand.

Dana parked Big Red and she climbed out of the Jeep. Qué Vista was one of hers and Benny's favorite restaurants. It sat right on the shoreline, with about half a dozen tables right on the white, sandy beach. The restaurant served a mixture of Tico cuisine for the locals and adventurous tourists as well as hamburgers and grilled cheese sandwiches that appealed to the tourists from up north who weren't too keen on the staples of the coastal Costa Rican diets: rice, beans, plantains, and fish. The restaurant also smartly had a bevy of vegetarian options to cater to the plethora of tourists that came to visit one of the popular yoga retreats that dotted the coast in the Nicoya Peninsula, which was a popular destination for yogi tourists. Mariposa Beach alone had several yoga retreats. The Jai Das Center for Peace and Relaxation was the largest and most popular one and was located right behind Dana's property a few clicks up the mountain.

Dana walked up the front steps into the restaurant and was

greeted by a smiling Jorge Granados, who was the head waiter and right-hand man of owner, María Rivera.

"Good evening, Doña Dana," Jorge said.

"Hi, Jorge. Beautiful night."

"It sure is. We're closing soon, but I'd be happy to get an order in right away before they close up the kitchen," Jorge said.

"Actually, I'm just looking for someone. I saw their truck parked out front," Dana said, looking around, not seeing them in the main part of the restaurant, which resembled a very large open gazebo offering direct views of the ocean a mere fifty feet away. Dana craned her neck down to the shoreline, where several tables right on the beach were the most popular with tourists. She spotted Cheyenne with a man. Dana figured that was her producer.

"I see them on the beach, thank you, Jorge."

"My pleasure. Let me know if you need anything to drink or if you change your mind about dinner. The kitchen won't close for another ten to fifteen minutes."

The tables on the beach were under a large open-sided palapa. They had strung outdoor patio lights throughout the thatched roof of the palapa, which was made of dried palm leaves. There were also several bamboo tiki torches staked right into the sand. It provided a calming tropical vibe, while its citronella torch kept the mosquitoes at bay. It was a beautiful spot at night, as if mystical forest fairies illuminated it. The sounds of the crashing waves a few feet away made the dinner experience out there even more special than back inside the main part of the restaurant.

Cheyenne picked the chair that faced toward the ocean, so her back was toward Dana as she approached their table. She saw the man bop his head toward Dana, literally giving Cheyenne a heads-up she was approaching.

Cheyenne turned around and smiled. "Hey, so glad you

stopped by."

As soon as Dana reached the table, Jorge appeared seemingly out of nowhere with a chair for Dana.

"Thank you, Jorge," Dana said, sitting.

"My pleasure, Doña Dana," Jorge said, scurrying away back toward the main building of the restaurant.

A busboy appeared to take away Cheyenne's and Nick's empty plates away.

"How was dinner?" Dana asked.

"It was lovely. I had the shrimp and rice with fried yucca. Delicious."

"That's one of my favorites here," Dana said.

"Nick had that whole fried-fish meal. What a sight, I didn't realize they actually brought out the whole fish, even its head and tail right on the plate."

"I'm still not used to that. It's weird to eat my meal with the fish staring back at me," Dana said.

"It was delicious. I'm Nick Suárez, by the way."

"So sorry, how rude of me. Nick is my producer and audio whiz. He's the reason my podcasts sound as good as they do."

"Nice to meet you."

"Likewise. I'm jealous that you actually moved down here. It's paradise," Nick said, looking around.

"San Francisco was getting to be too much for me. I needed a change of scenery, so I jumped at the chance."

"I can see why they call this place Qué Vista," Cheyenne said, looking out to the ocean. Qué Vista was Spanish for What a View.

Jorge stopped by to see if anyone was interested in dessert.

"I sure am," Cheyenne said. "Will you join us for dessert?"

Dana nodded. "Sure, thank you. I'll have the Tres Leches and an espresso. Sleep be darned tonight."

"Oh boy, I love tres leches. I'll have the same," Nick said.

"Well, sounds like a ringing endorsement. Make it three tres leches, my good man," Cheyenne said, smiling.

While they waited for their desserts, Cheyenne turned to the topic of the podcast.

"Did you get a chance to talk to Benny? I was sort of hoping to see him join us."

"Are we still off the record?"

Cheyenne and Nick both smiled.

"Of course."

"Good. I talked to Benny, but he's still on the fence about all this. He's a lawyer, so his first instinct is to clam up. The less said, the better is sort of his mantra in these types of things," Dana said.

"I get it. But this podcast only works if I can get to the truth, which might vindicate Benny once and for all. It must be hard for him to have this case lingering over his head for all these years," Cheyenne said.

"But he... we... aren't sure if we can really trust you. No offense, but your goal here is to put out a successful, titillating podcast, not to clear Benny's name," Dana said.

"No offense taken, and thank you for being so frank. It's refreshing. And you're right. The podcast is my number-one priority. But I think our end goals are aligned, Dana."

"Do you think Ed North is dead?" Dana asked.

"I do."

"You think he was murdered?"

"Yes, again."

"Who do you think killed him?"

Cheyenne looked over at Nick, who shrugged. She leaned to get closer to Dana.

"Off the record, of course," Cheyenne said with a wink and big smile. "If I were the gambling type, my money would be on Terri."

Dana believed her.

"She's the prime suspect with the Florida authorities, but they haven't been able to charge her. It's an uphill battle without a body, and the fact that it's now been seven years since he vanished makes things even tougher for the detectives."

"I'm assuming you've done a lot of investigative research into this case as you prepared for the podcast," Dana said.

"I have fifty plus hours of research, so far."

"That's impressive. I'm assuming you have access to info well beyond Google," Dana said.

Cheyenne smiled. "I'm proud of my research skills. That's how I got started in this business. I was a researcher and fact-checker for a couple network shows. For this show, I got access to the case files from the cold-case detective in Miami and the OIJ case files."

Dana lit up. "You did? You've seen the OIJ reports?"

Cheyenne smiled and nodded.

The OIJ were the Spanish initials for the Organismo de Investigación Judicial—the Judicial Investigation National Police. They were the FBI's equivalent in Costa Rica.

Dana was about to pepper Cheyenne with questions, but Jorge arrived with the tres leches cake slices. Fresh strawberries sat on top of the deliciously moist cake. Tres leches literally meant three milks in Spanish. It was a butter cake that was soaked in evaporated milk, condensed milk, and heavy cream. They then chilled it in the refrigerator and served cold.

Dana, Cheyenne, and Nick admired the pretty presentation before they tore into the scrumptious treat.

"What can you share about the OIJ report regarding Benny?" Dana asked after a few bites of her dessert.

Cheyenne put her fork down. "Like I said earlier, I admire your honesty and direct approach, so I'll do the same. It doesn't look good for Benny, I'm afraid."

Chapter Ten

DANA WOKE up early the next morning. She'd slept terribly, tossing and turning all night with Cheyenne's words playing in her head on a never-ending auto loop: *It doesn't look good for Benny, I'm afraid.*

The tossing and turning got so bad that at around two a.m. Wally hissed at her and jumped off the bed to find a better spot to get his hard-earned twenty hours of sleep. She blamed the restless and sleepless night not just on what Cheyenne had told her about the police report on Benny, but on the late-night sugar overdose, courtesy of the tres leches cake and the caffeine kick of the espresso. It was frightening knowing that the police suspected Benny for the disappearance of Ed North. Benny had told Dana that he was certain that was the case, but to have it confirmed by Cheyenne, who had seen the actual police case files, put it into a whole other nightmarish level.

The case had long gone cold. The OIJ didn't have a dedicated cold-case squad like they have in many police departments back in the States, so she wasn't sure how hard they had been working on Ed North's disappearance over the last few years. She assumed they had put it on the back burner. But

Cheyenne's podcast was going to bring a lot of attention to it, and it was going to embarrass the OIJ for not having resolved it, so she figured after the podcast they were going to throw everything they had at the case with Benny as their prime suspect.

Cheyenne indicated the OIJ had taken a long, hard look at Terri, but she was thousands of miles away in Florida when Ed went missing. Her alibi checked out. It was airtight. *Could Terri really be innocent?* Dana thought.

Cheyenne seemed to believe Terri was still a prime suspect, since there wasn't any proof that Ed had made it to Costa Rica. He was flying his own airplane, so he didn't clear regular customs like most tourists entering the country. A paper visa wasn't needed for Americans; they just had to leave the country within ninety days.

The only so-called proof that Ed was coming to Costa Rica was Terri's statement to the Miami Police Department.

Terri hadn't bothered to report her husband missing, saying she wasn't expecting him for another couple of weeks. It was one of Ed's daughters who filed the missing persons report with the police after two weeks of not being able to get a hold of her dad, which was very unusual since they were close. It was only then that Terri filed her own missing persons report.

But even after filing, the Miami police noted in their reports that Terri didn't seem worried about her husband's whereabouts, noting that Terri said it wasn't unusual for them not to communicate over the phone or the internet when he was in Costa Rica. She actually seemed to be bothered by their investigation for intruding in her life more than anything else.

Dana would have loved to get her hands on those reports, but Cheyenne put the kibosh on it, saying she couldn't share anything she got from her sources. It frustrated Dana, but as a former journalist herself, she understood.

Having grown tired of tossing and turning and kicking off

the covers when it got too hot, only to get back under them when it seemed the temperature dropped, Dana climbed out of bed at six thirty and walked out to the veranda to smell the fresh air. It was overcast, but there was a mugginess to the air. She was actually looking forward to the midafternoon rain showers. Down below in the vegetable garden she saw Ramón Villalobos, who was the property's caretaker, already tending to the garden. He was wielding his trusty machete on the yuca plants, digging up that waxy, delicious yuca root for later.

It had been a strange proposition when she inherited Casa Verde from her uncle, who made it a condition that Ramón and his wife, Carmen, would remain in their home on the property and continue as Casa Verde's caretaker. For a city girl from San Francisco, it was a strange concept to have live-in caretakers, but a year since moving she couldn't imagine living there without Ramón and Carmen.

She went back into the bedroom to get ready for the day. Wally came sauntering over from who knows where in the house. He looked at Dana, then at the empty bed. He yawned, stretched, and jumped onto the bed, laying in the warm spot she had left.

"Bum," Dana said. She grabbed her phone and called Benny, knowing that he would already be on the road back to Escazú, but he didn't pick up. She checked for a text message from him, but there were none.

"Strange," she said out loud to herself. Benny always texted her when he hit the road and when he arrived in Escazú. Perhaps he'd left really early and didn't want the text message to wake her. She also supposed that with the stress of this Ed North mess crashing back into his life and with a client meeting he had scheduled in the morning, he must have been too preoccupied and had forgotten to text her. Dana tossed the phone on her bed. Wally looked up from his sleep, giving her an *excuse me, I'm sleeping here* look.

"Sorry, bum," she said. She contemplated going on a run, but she wasn't feeling it, so she went to her bathroom and drew a bath. She would soak for a while, then have breakfast and coffee before heading to the bookstore.

Thirty minutes later, she had finished bathing and had toweled off and gotten dressed. She slipped on her usual, a boxy white T-shirt and khaki shorts. She checked her phone. Benny still hadn't called or texted. She made her ways downstairs and made some oatmeal, scooping in a bit of brown sugar and some fruit on top. She ate her oatmeal and drank coffee while she perused her usual social media haunts on her phone.

The phone buzzed in her hand, startling her. She was hoping to see Benny's name flashing on the caller ID, but it wasn't him. It was Cheyenne Lively. Dana took the call.

"What's up?"

"Have you heard the news?" Cheyenne asked.

"No, what's going on?" Dana said, feeling a little embarrassed for the slow, lazy start of her day.

"Terri Kaminski is dead," Cheyenne said.

Dana wasn't sure what language Cheyenne was using since what she said made little sense. It sounded like English... but what had she said?

"What do you mean, she's dead?" *What a stupid question*, Dana thought as soon as she asked it.

"She's dead. Her husband, who called the police, found her body."

"When?"

"About two hours ago."

Dana couldn't believe what she had heard.

"She was murdered, Dana," Cheyenne said.

"Murdered?"

"Yes. I don't have all the details yet, but the police and CSI people are on the scene as we speak."

Oh my word, Dana thought, feeling lightheaded.

"Have you talked to Benny this morning?"

"No. He was heading up to the city earlier in the morning. Why do you ask that?"

"My police source told me he's a person of interest in her murder."

Dana stood there in shocked silence. She didn't know long she stood there, but it must have been longer than she thought, as Cheyenne's voice broke her from that stupor.

"Dana, are you there? Hello? Are you okay?"

"Sorry. Yes, I'm here. I just can't... I just can't believe she's dead and that the police want to pin her death on Benny too. I need to call Benny." Dana hung up and immediately dialed Benny's number, wondering why she hadn't heard a peep from him in almost twenty-four hours.

Chapter Eleven

BENNY PICKED up on the first ring. *Thank God*, Dana thought when she heard his voice.

"Benny, thank goodness, I was getting worried."

"Sorry for being MIA, sweetheart. I've had a crazy morning. I couldn't find my cell phone. Had to tear the car apart until I finally found it between the passenger seat and the console. Battery was dead, so I had to charge it. I was going to call you on the landline, but I had to get ready for my client meeting this morning."

"That's okay, I was just worried, since you always text to let me know you got in safely."

"Didn't mean to worry you."

"I just got off the phone with Cheyenne Lively. Something terrible has happened."

"Is this about Terri's death?"

"Yes. How did you hear about it up there already?"

"An OIJ investigator from San José showed up at my house first thing this morning," Benny said.

"Oh dear, how did that go?"

"Could have gone better. Since I'm considered a person of

interest in her first husband's disappearance and Terri was my prime accuser and now she turns up murdered, well, I just earned the top spot on their list of suspects," Benny said. He sounded much calmer than she would be if the shoe were on her foot.

"Oh my gosh, Benny. What are you going to do?"

"I'm still processing all of this, so I don't know. I have two client meetings today and a closing, so I need to focus on that right now. Gives me time to figure out what the heck is going on and what my next move will be."

"Okay. But what did the police say, exactly?"

"They wanted to know where I was between midnight and five this morning, which I suppose is the time window the medical examiner has given for Terri's death. So I told them I went to bed at nine thirty. Woke up at four and hit the road at four thirty. The fact that I was alone and no one can corroborate that didn't score me any points."

"You were with me, Benny."

"You left at nine. They only care about that midnight-to-five time range. And I was alone during that time."

"What can I do to help?"

"Nothing for now. I'll figure this out. I'm innocent, so I'm not worried. But I need to get going. I'll call you this afternoon."

Dana put the phone down. She sat on her kitchen island counter, dumbfounded. Wally must have sensed her state of mind, so he jumped on the counter to comfort her. Dana smiled as she rubbed his little rump as he stretched and purred in delight, making her feel slightly better.

After a few minutes of utter shock, Dana sprang into action. She was not one to sit around waiting for news. She called Gabriela Rojas.

Gabriela Rojas was a police detective with the OIJ based out of Nicoya, which was the nearest town of size in the province. The closest OIJ station was located there, about fifty miles from Mariposa Beach. Dana was on friendly terms with Detective Rojas, but she couldn't say the same about Rojas's partner and boss, Jorge Picado. Gabriela picked up on the first ring, startling Dana.

"Dana. I was just going to call you," Rojas said. Dana didn't like the sound of that.

"Really. What about?"

"For the same reason you're calling me this early in the morning."

"Terri Kaminski," Dana whispered.

"Are you going to be in town this afternoon?"

"Yes. Why? What's up?" Dana was taking a page from Benny's playbook: the less said, the better. Especially when talking to the police.

"We're headed down to Mariposa Beach right now. We'll need to chat in the afternoon."

"Official police stuff?"

"I'm afraid so."

"What the heck is going on, Gabriela?"

"Your name has come up during the investigation."

"My name? Why?"

"Do you know Terri Kaminski?"

"I didn't know her. I met her once, yesterday, at my bookstore."

"You had a confrontation with her?"

"I wouldn't describe it that way. She was upset and yelled at me, but that was about it. I hardly got a word in before Leo asked her to leave."

"Okay. Just make sure you're at the bookstore around two this afternoon. We'll sort things out," Rojas said.

Dana stood there, stunned for a moment. Things were getting hairy. She figured Terri's new husband, Burt, told the

OIJ about their encounter with Terri. And now Rojas and Picado were coming to town.

Gabriela Rojas and Juan Mora Picado were the OIJ investigators assigned to the small beach towns on the Nicoya Peninsula. Most of the OIJ detectives worked out of larger towns and cities, and they disliked coming down to the off the beaten track small beach towns.

The law enforcement presence out on the coast was rather minimal. It was under the purview of the National Police Force of Costa Rica and mostly patrolled by cops from its Tourist Police division.

Tourism police officers usually got around on bicycles or on motocross motorcycles, cheerfully interacting with tourists who were lost or had their backpack stolen from the beach. For murder and other serious crimes, the Tourist Police and all other uniformed police forces in the country had to step aside for the agents of the elite OIJ. They were the only ones with investigative powers and with the power to charge someone with a crime in the country.

Dana had a history with Jorge Picado, and it wasn't a good one. They got along like cats and dogs. She imagined the ornery detective was already upset at having to make the hour-long drive down to Mariposa Beach, but having Dana's name pop up in the investigation once again probably made his head spin.

Dana checked the time. It was eight. The bookstore side of the cafe didn't open until nine thirty, but Mindy and Leo opened the coffeehouse at seven to appease the caffeine seekers, so Dana decided to head over there. She would have one of Mindy's bagel breakfast sandwiches and coffee. She wanted to know if the OIJ had talked to Mindy and Leo, since they had exchanged words with Terri as well. And what about Cheyenne? She'd been there too.

Dana called Cheyenne as she got ready to leave.

After saying hello, Dana asked her if she had heard from the police.

"I received a call from an Agent Picado. He was a barrel of laughs," Cheyenne said sarcastically.

"I know him well, and he's always unpleasant," Dana said.

"He knew about our little encounter with Terri yesterday," Cheyenne said.

"Yeah, I just got off the phone with Picado's partner, Gabriela Rojas, telling me as much."

"I'm sure Burt Kaminski was more than happy to give the police our names and to tell them about our confrontation."

"Why would Burt do that?"

"Whenever a spouse is murdered, the police zero in on the surviving spouse. I'm sure the police are all over him, so he's giving them other options."

"What the heck is going on, Cheyenne?"

"I don't know, but I'm going to find out."

Chapter Twelve

DANA ARRIVED at the bookstore slash cafe fifteen minutes after talking to Cheyenne. Although she still didn't trust her, she felt a sense of relief that an experienced investigative journalist with her impressive track record of cracking cold cases was doing her own investigation about what was going on.

Mindy greeted Dana with a hug.

"Did the OIJ call you?"

Mindy nodded. "Agent Picado called me this morning. He said that Leo and I needed to be here in the early afternoon for questioning on the Terri Kaminski case."

Dana noticed how Picado had called everyone but her, giving that job to Rojas. Dana chuckled, thinking about that. Cats and dogs, indeed.

"Do you know what happened to that lady?" Mindy asked. Her face was awash with worry.

"Lady? You're being kind," Leo said, interrupting them.

"I wouldn't say that to the detectives," Dana said.

"I got nothing to hide. She's not the first rude customer I've kicked out of here and banned. Won't be the last either. People are so darn entitled nowadays," Leo said.

"Please, hon, we shouldn't talk about the dead that way. It's bad luck," Mindy said. The superstition vibe was always strong with her. Mindy turned to Dana. "What do you think about all this?"

"That this is an ugly mess. I would imagine this all ties back to Ed North somehow, and I'm going to figure out how."

"Don't stick your nose into Picado's investigation again, Dana. You know how much he hates that," Leo warned.

"I'm just curious," Dana said. "And I wonder..." Dana trailed off as she headed toward her back office.

"There goes trouble," Leo said as Mindy tossed a few eye grenades his way.

Back in her office, she went through her security video footage from the last twenty-four hours. One of Benny's friends was in security, so he had installed a top-of-the-line security system that seemed way over the top to Dana. On her computer, she accessed video camera footage which kept its keen eye inside the bookstore slash cafe and out front and the back alley, which was mostly used for deliveries. She cued up the time of Terri and Burt's arrival and there was the footage—the video image crisp in HD and the audio clear as day. Dana knew the OIJ would want that footage. She watched Terri going bat crazy yesterday. It was so bizarre. That lively firecracker on the video cussing and fussing everyone out and demanding signatures of NDAs was dead. No longer around to rant and rave. Dana spent the next hour glued to the monitor. Amalfi Soto brought her a bagel with mango cream cheese and a big-gulp-size cup of coffee. She had forgotten to eat.

"Thank you, Amalfi, you're the best."

She continued going through the video while eating and drinking coffee.

The bagel was long gone, and she had just about drained the last of the coffee into her belly when something on the video feed caught her eye. It was the camera facing Main Street. She saw some familiar faces, Big Mike heading into his surf shop. José Luis, the self-appointed security guard of the parking lot out front at his post. Ernesto Castro, the pulpería owner walking toward his convenience store. And then those people she didn't know who weren't the locals. They were the rainy-season tourists heading into her bookstore slash cafe or visiting one of the other vendors on Ark Row or heading down toward the beach in their flip-flops.

But there was one older gentleman that was sticking out because he seemed to hang outside of the bookstore. A lot. She thought little of it the first few times she saw him, but he kept showing up on video. Just standing there looking toward Dana's store, like one of those morning television show fans who hang out on the other side of the glass, staring into the camera, hoping for a glimpse of Savannah Guthrie and Al Roker. He was the only one that stood out after she spent over two hours sifting through the video recordings.

Something else made the stranger stand out: He looked familiar, but she couldn't place the man. She sent the clip to herself so as to later show Cheyenne and see if she and that producer tech whiz could do more with the video.

Dana felt cooped up after spending all that time in her small office going over the video surveillance, so she was about to go out for a walk on the beach when she looked down at the live video feed on the monitors from out front and saw the white sedan parking. She recognized it as Picado and Rojas's car. It was an unmarked car, but it screamed OIJ.

She saw the two investigators getting out of the car, the

mustached Picado with his black hair combed to the right, while Rojas had her long, black hair pulled back. She looked up at the camera as if she knew Dana was watching them. They were early.

"Great. Just what I need right now. The third degree from Picado," Dana said out loud, even though she was alone in her office. *Might as well get it over with*, she thought as she got up and walked out of her office into the bookstore to greet the two detectives, figuring Picado would be as salty and crusty as usual.

After a curt greeting, Picado said he would interview Mindy and Leo, leaving Rojas to talk with Dana. So they went back to the office.

"There isn't much to say," Dana said when Rojas asked her to walk her through what had happened between her and Terri Kaminski. She had her phone out to record the conversation.

"Just start from the beginning. I want to hear it all, even if you think it's something small and not important, okay?" Rojas said.

"Sure. I was chatting with Cheyenne Lively."

"The podcaster doing that show on Ed North?" Rojas asked.

Dana nodded. "That's right." Then she told Rojas about how Terri and her husband, Burt, walked into the store as she was walking Cheyenne out and how Terri became upset when she saw them together.

"She read me the riot act," Dana said.

"And that was the first time you had ever talked with the Kaminskis?"

"First and only. But Mr. Kaminski didn't say much. Terri was the one who kept going on and on about us trying to railroad her with the podcast in order to get Benny off the hook."

"Then what happened?"

"Terri wanted us to sign these NDA agreements. She wanted everyone in the store to sign them. We all refused, which got her even more upset. She was out of control. Began cussing, so Leo finally nipped it in the bud and asked her to leave before he called the police. It took a couple more tries, but she finally took the advice and stormed out in a huff."

"What is your involvement with that podcast?"

"I have no involvement. Cheyenne wants to interview Benny, since he was Ed North's lawyer when he disappeared. He had refused, so she wanted me to change his mind."

"Did you?"

Dana shrugged. "Well, yeah. I mean, there is a cloud over him with this whole Ed North deal, and it's only going to get worse with this popular podcast taking on the Ed North case. So maybe it could help clear his name."

"So he agreed to talk with Ms. Lively?"

"That was just last night, and he had to go back to the city for work. So he was thinking it over."

"All right," Rojas said, putting her phone in her pocket and getting up to leave.

Before they could make it out the door, the lead investigator, Jorge Picado, walked in. It was a small office to begin with, but three people—one of them being Jorge Picado—made Dana feel claustrophobic.

"I just finished talking with Dana," Rojas said. Picado stood there for a moment or two, his black, steely eyes boring into Dana.

"One question, Ms. Kirkpatrick," Picado said. It seemed to Dana that saying her name left a nasty taste in his mouth.

The two of them had quite the history. In the year since Dana had moved to Mariposa Beach, they had crossed paths several times. The first time was when her cousin, who contested her inheritance of Casa Verde in the courts, was murdered. Picado was the lead investigator, and he made Dana his prime suspect. It was an awful feeling, one she wanted to ensure Benny didn't have to contend with for long. Even though she was proven innocent and the actual murderer of her cousin was discovered, Picado never apologized. She supposed it was hard for him to admit he was wrong.

Picado continued speaking. "Mr. Campos states you were the last person to see him last night."

"That's right. I had dinner at his place. I left around nine."

"Is that normal for you to go to your own place? I thought you were a couple."

"That's none of your business," Dana snapped. She regretted the harshness of her tone, but that seemed out of line. Dana looked at Rojas, who looked away.

"Mr. Campos claims he left Mariposa Beach at four in the morning to head up to San José. It's unusual to leave so early since we checked and he didn't have a meeting in San José with a client until later in the day."

"He wanted to beat traffic, so that's normal. He'll leave at four in the morning or ten at night. Anything to avoid getting stuck on the highway behind a convey of big-rig trucks blowing exhaust down at you," Dana said.

That seemed to satisfy Picado. Everyone understood that traffic avoidance was a big part of living in Costa Rica.

"All right. That's it for now," Picado said, putting away his notebook.

"What happened to Terri, anyway? When was she killed?"

"That is none of *your* business," Picado said. It sounded as if he were hissing. And he even cracked a smirk. *I guess you got me back, doofus*, Dana thought, but she said nothing more. He was out the door. That was a win in her book.

Chapter Thirteen

AFTER PICADO AND ROJAS LEFT, Dana went to check how Mindy, Leo, and Amalfi had fared under the questioning from the surly detective.

"It went fine. There wasn't much to tell," Mindy said.

"That's what I told Gabriela. Terri came in here, yelled at us, threatened us with NDAs and then we kicked her out because she was so belligerent," Dana said.

"That's what we told Picado," Leo said.

"I need to get out of here," Dana said.

"Are you going to be all right?" a worried Mindy asked.

"I'll be fine. I'll see you tomorrow."

Dana went home, leaving Amalfi in charge of the bookstore. She didn't tell Mindy what she was planning to do, since that would just worry her friend. As she drove Big Red, she called Cheyenne Lively and asked her if she could come to Casa Verde to talk about what had been going on. Cheyenne agreed to be there in thirty minutes.

Dana hung up as she pulled into her long driveway, surrounded by Ramón Villalobos's master gardening skills. Tropical flowers and fruit trees bearing bananas, cas, avocados, and mangoes surrounded the driveway. She saw Ramón and Carmen working on their new hobby, chickens. Ramón had asked Dana if it was okay to corral a patch of land for chickens. She was thrilled, dreaming of fresh eggs. She stopped the Jeep to say hello.

"Wow, you guys are doing a fantastic job," Dana said, admiring the cedar chicken coop they had been building.

"It's coming along," Ramón said, smiling proudly. "The chickens will have a cozy indoor nesting box and a large courtyard space while they're in the coop, so they come in and out during the day. But at night they will be able to sleep safe from the raccoons, the coatis, opossums, owls, and foxes."

"A few more days and we'll be able to start bring the chickens home to roost," Carmen added.

"I hope Wally doesn't become one of the chickens' predators," Dana said about her adopted cat.

"I'm not worried about him. That kitty has been hanging around before you moved in, and I never had a problem when we've had other critters running around," Ramón said.

"But I'll keep an eye on the little rascal," Carmen said, smiling.

"Me too," Dana said. She waved goodbye and drove up the house.

Dana went inside and was greeted by Wally.

"Don't you try to eat those new chickens that will be moving in soon," Dana said, scratching behind his ear. He meowed gently. She could almost hear him saying, *Who, me?*

"Okay, you sweet talker, I trust you."

She went into the kitchen and had a glass of fresh-squeezed cas juice from the fruits right outside. She had never even heard of the small, green fruit until she moved to Costa Rica, discovering that cas was delicious with its tart flavor.

She called Benny, but he didn't pick up. A few minutes

later, he texted her: *Sorry, client meeting soon then visiting Beatrice. Call you tonight.*

She was upset by the blow-off, but she understood. He was busy with work and excited to visit his daughter, Beatrice. Dating a father had made her nervous at first. Being the girlfriend to a tween's dad conjured a lot of negative images from television and the movies. But Beatrice was a sweet girl. And they got along well enough, although they didn't spend much time together, as Beatrice lived with her mother in Escazú.

Benny said it was a battle to tear Beatrice away from the mall and her friends to come to middle-of-nowhere Mariposa Beach. Dana figured the poor girl probably wasn't too keen to spend the weekend with her dad and his girlfriend, to boot.

Cheyenne Lively and Nick Suárez arrived at Casa Verde at six. She offered them cas juice, which they accepted and loved.

"Wow, never had this before," Cheyenne said, drinking it up.

"Have you had the talk with Detective Picado?" Dana asked.

Cheyenne and Nick exchanged glances.

"We did earlier today. We had the pleasure of meeting Mr. Sunshine in person," Cheyenne said facetiously.

Dana laughed.

"Has he always been a curmudgeon?" Cheyenne asked.

"I've only been here a year, and he's always been that way, and the old ladies from the Gossip Brigade say he's been ornery since he was a kid growing up nearby," Dana said.

"Gossip Brigade?"

"Don't worry, you'll meet them soon enough."

"Ah, gotta love the small-town living," Cheyenne said with a smile. Dana looked at her, puzzled.

"I live in LA but grew up in a small town in Nebraska."

"So you know how quickly word gets around in a small town," Dana said.

"I sure do."

"Anyway, Picado is always unpleasant but doesn't care for me much, so that goes double for me," Dana said.

"I doubt he cares about most people."

"So what did he ask you?" Dana asked.

"About Terri and Burt and our little confrontation. He also wanted to know what I was doing here. How long I was staying. I told him as long as it takes."

"As long as what takes?" Dana asked.

"That's what he asked too. To solve the Ed North cold case."

"How did he take that?"

"Not. Good," Cheyenne said, following with a laugh. Nick just shook his head, used to getting into awkward situations with Cheyenne while on the job.

"He pushed me to give up what I had come up with in my investigation of the Ed North case, but I told him to go fly a kite."

"I think I might have just moved down to number two on his blacklist," Dana said, chuckling.

"I know the First Amendment only applies in the US, but Costa Rica has press freedom laws in place, so I gave him the name of the network's lawyer if he has a problem with it."

"Oh boy, that must have gotten his socks in a bunch." Dana felt petty, but she couldn't help but take a little joy in hearing how Cheyenne had manhandled Picado, since he had been so nasty to her since they'd first met.

Cheyenne then turned more serious. "He asked me about

Benny."

"I figured as much. He seems to circle his wagons around him. What did you say?"

"The truth. I never met the man. We've exchanged a few emails. I talked to him once on the phone and he told me he didn't want to talk to me about the case and blocked me on the mobile and social media. So I had nothing to tell him about Benny." After a moment of awkward silence, Cheyenne spoke up once again. "Has Benny come around to taking to me?"

Dana shook her head. "No. And he's been shutting me out since he left Mariposa Beach," Dana said. Her eyes were getting watery, and she felt embarrassed.

"He's dealing with a lot of pressure, I'm sure," Cheyenne said.

"I came across something interesting," Dana said, eager to change the subject.

"What's that?"

"I was going through my video surveillance footage from the bookstore yesterday around the time Terri and Burt showed up, and I noticed there was a strange man that seemed to hang around the store across the street. A lot. I got that stalker-ish vibe, seeing him there gawking toward the bookstore all day."

"Let's take a look," Cheyenne said.

Dana led Cheyenne and Nick to her laptop on the kitchen island. She flipped it open and clicked on the clip of the video she had saved to show them.

"Here you go," she said, sliding the laptop toward Cheyenne. Nick stood over her shoulder, watching with interest.

"Shut the front door," Cheyenne said, getting closer to the laptop's monitor.

"Do you know him?" Dana asked.

"I'm not sure, but... he looks like Ed North."

Chapter Fourteen

Dana was dumbfounded. Could Ed North really be alive?

She had given Nick Suárez access to her security footage. He said he would investigate it further with the DEQ Network experts who worked in this type of stuff by using facial-recognition software. Dana had heard about that before, and it sounded like a privacy-invading creepy stuff George Orwell might have dreamed up, but if it could help Benny, she was up for it.

Benny still hadn't called her back, which had her worried. He had never been this uncommunicative toward her. She had gotten closer to him the last six months, feeling that they made a good team, a couple with honest communication. Yet he'd never shared the story about Ed North with her until now, and he wasn't really sharing it with her. He was forced to. And he was being cagey about it. But she didn't want to go down the road of suspicion. Benny was Ed North's lawyer, so there were client-lawyer privileges he couldn't just open up to her willy-nilly.

Dana couldn't stop thinking about Terri Kaminski. She had been saying for years that either Ed had started a new life somewhere else in secret or they'd killed him because of a shady business deal in Costa Rica with Benny. Even though most fingers pointed to her as her husband's killer, if that really was Ed North prowling outside the bookstore, could Terri have been telling the truth all these years about her innocence in his disappearance?

Had Ed started a new life in Costa Rica? And maybe that was why Benny didn't want to talk about it. As his lawyer, maybe Benny helped him start a new life in the tropics. But it made little sense to Dana. If Ed North wanted to start over far away from Terri, why would he remain hidden and let her declare him dead for her to claim his estate and leave his other family—his first wife and kids—cut off from his vast estate? And what was he doing for money? There weren't a lot of job opportunities for a sixty something American expat.

Dana kept looking at the still of the old man in the video. She compared it to pictures of Ed North. There were similarities, but it was hard to know for sure if that man in the video was Ed North.

If Ed North did successfully vanish and start a new life for all these years, why come back now? Did he find out about Terri? Did he feel he was forced to come out of hiding and back to Mariposa Beach to kill her? It was too much for Dana. Her head was spinning.

Dana took a nice, long bath while reading a novel. She drank a glass of wine and nestled into bed with Wally. She would read until she dozed off. It must have worked like a charm, because suddenly the jarring sound of her phone ringing startled her awake. She had put the ringer up to the highest setting to ensure she wouldn't miss a call from Benny, but in the dead of night, fast asleep, the loud ringtone made her jump out of bed as if it were on fire. She assumed it was Benny, but it was not the ringtone she had assigned to him, so she checked the time: 11:20 p.m. Who would call this late? It couldn't be good news.

"Hello?"

"Hi, Dana, it's Beatrice. Sorry for calling so late." Dana was surprised to receive a call from Benny's daughter. They got along well and all, but they never chatted on the phone, especially if Benny wasn't in town.

"It's fine. Is everything all right?"

"No," Beatrice said as she started crying.

Oh no, something terrible must have happened to Benny. An accident?

"What is it, honey? Is your dad okay?"

"They arrested him."

The room spun.

"Who arrested him? For what?"

"The OIJ. They picked him up this afternoon at his office and they put him in jail."

"What for?"

"I don't know. My mom won't tell me. But I wanted to tell you so would know and because I know you'll help my dad get out of jail," Beatrice said amid sobs.

"You bet your bottom dollar, Beatrice. I'll find out what's going on and I'll help your dad. We both know he's a good, honest man, so whatever is going on, it's a mistake. So he'll be home soon, don't you worry."

"Do you promise?"

"I promise," Dana said without hesitation.

After hanging up with Beatrice, Dana hoped she hadn't made a promise she couldn't keep.

She was certain the police had picked Benny up because of this whole mess with Ed and Terri. In Costa Rica, they had something called preventive detention, which was the practice of incarcerating individuals before trial. This was usually done if they were worried that a suspect might flee or commit other crimes while free, awaiting for trial. Preventive detention required a judge's order. Dana couldn't imagine what the police had found against him that would have convinced a judge to issue an order of preventive detention so soon. At this hour, her options were limited. She scrolled through her phone for Detective Gabriela Rojas's phone number and called it. Rojas picked up on the third ring. She didn't sound like she had been roused out of bed by the late call.

"Gabriela, sorry for calling so late," Dana said.

"It's all right. You must have heard about Benny," Rojas said matter-of-factly.

"His daughter just called me in tears. What's going on?"

"You know I can't get into the details of a police investigation. But he was arrested a few hours ago in the case related to Terri Kaminski's death."

"You have to be kidding."

"Afraid I'm not. There has been some new evidence, and Picado thought it warranted he be arrested, so he asked the OIJ in San José to pick him up."

"Is this under preventive detention?"

"You're getting to know our legal system well, but no, not yet. Picado is working on that for the morning, so right now he can only be held for twenty-four hours without a court order."

"I know you can't get into the nitty-gritty with me, but do you think Picado has enough to get that court order?"

It took a moment for Rojas to mull it over. Dana could just about see her thinking it over whether she should say anything more. But unlike Picado, with whom she had a frosty relationship, she and Gabriela had developed a friendly acquaintance.

"I do. Get Benny a good criminal defense lawyer, Dana. Goodnight."

Dana held the phone with the dead line in her hand for a moment, her mouth agape as she cried.

Chapter Fifteen

DANA GOT three hours of sleep, which actually surprised her. Her first call that morning was to Shirley Pacheco. Benny had given her a list of people to contact if she ever needed help with legal matters, if he wasn't around or for parts of the legal system out of his wheelhouse like criminal law—Benny was a real estate attorney. He didn't do criminal law work—so months ago, when Dana got into a legal jam and Picado was threatening her with preventive detention, Benny had told her that if she was picked up, she needed to call Shirley Pacheco, one of the best criminal defense lawyers in the country. The receptionist put Dana through to Shirley.

"Good morning, Dana. I was actually getting ready to call you," Pacheco said.

"About Benny, I assume?"

"That's right. He called me as soon as they arrested him. I've taken his case and I'm working right now to get him out of holding."

"That's wonderful. Benny told me you're the best criminal lawyer in the country," Dana said, feeling buoyed with hope for the first time since Beatrice's call.

"Rest assured, I'll be providing the best defense I can offer. He wanted me to call you to assure you that he's doing okay under the circumstances. They're limiting his phone access. But he was concerned, knowing you would be worried sick by now."

Dana's heart melted. He was sitting in jail and was concerned about her wellbeing.

"What is going on, Shirley?"

"Benny told me I could talk to you freely, so I'll share what I know so far. Bear in mind, I'm just digging my heels into the case this morning, but the police claim to have enough evidence to prove that Benny murdered Terri Kaminski."

Dana almost dropped her phone. "What? That's ridiculous."

"Right now there isn't a court order, so they can only hold him for another twelve hours. I need to see what this evidence is so I can start chipping away at it so that the judge won't grant the order to keep Benny in jail beyond the twenty-four-hour window. I'll keep you posted."

"Of course, thank you. I'll let you get to work."

"One thing, Dana. What do you know about Burt Kaminski?"

"Not much. I just know he's married to Terri. I only met them once a couple of days ago in my bookstore. But he didn't say much. He seemed to be henpecked by Terri."

"Well, he's the star witness against Benny."

For the second time in a few minutes, Dana almost dropped her phone on the floor. This case was getting more bizarre by the second.

"What would Burt have on Benny about anything?" Dana asked.

"I don't know, but I'm going to find out."

Dana's next call was to Cheyenne.

"Hi, Dana, I was meaning to call you. I'm so sorry about Benny's arrest."

"How on earth do you know about that already?" It seemed everyone knew Benny had been arrested but her.

"I have a source in the police."

"You do? What do you know?"

"You're not going to like it," Cheyenne said, sounding sheepish.

"Please tell me what you know."

"Okay. For starters, they found the murder weapon. It was a tire iron."

"Oh goodness," Dana said, feeling bad for the grisly demise of Terri Kaminski. The woman might have been nasty to her the one time they'd met, but no one deserved to be killed like that.

"It gets worse, I'm afraid."

"It's okay. I want to know everything that's going on."

"Dana..." There was a moment of silence, as if Cheyenne was mustering the courage to tell her something awful.

"The police found the tire iron, the murder weapon, in Benny's safe in his beach house."

That time, Dana did drop the phone.

It felt like she stood there in her kitchen for about an hour, but it was a few seconds until she picked up the phone from the floor. She could hear Cheyenne's voice through the speaker.

"Dana, are you there? Are you all right?"

Dana put the phone back to her ear. "Sorry, I dropped the phone."

"I'm sorry to give you such terrible news."

"It's a mistake. It makes little sense. Benny couldn't hurt a fly."

"Are you sure about that? You haven't known him that long, have you?"

Dana's stomach was already a mess; Cheyenne's comment

made her feel like there was a big line of people taking turns kicking her in the gut.

"I know he's not a killer, Cheyenne," Dana said coldly. Angry.

"I'm sorry. I didn't mean to make you more upset. It's just the journalist in me. You used to be a journalist, you remember how we're wired to think the worst in people."

"I was wired to find the truth."

"As am I, and that's all I'm trying to do here."

"You just want to put out your podcast and get a million downloads a minute with Benny starring as a tire iron–swinging maniac."

"I'm just after the truth, Dana. Wherever it takes me."

"I need to call Gabriela."

"As in Detective Gabriela Rojas?"

"Yes, tell her that there is no way she could believe Benny did this, and then what? Kept the murder weapon in a safe at home. It's ludicrous. Why not toss it into the ocean?"

"Dana, I told you this between us. Off the record, remember? If you go half-cocked to the police, they're going to want to know how you know stuff only the police would know at this juncture. The police will put up the pressure to plug leaks, so you could scare my source away. So I'm begging you, don't talk to the police. You'll only make things worse for Benny. And it's not like she's going to share any details about an ongoing investigation with you anyway," Cheyenne said.

Dana knew Cheyenne was right. No good would come of her calling Detective Rojas, especially with Picado usually within earshot of everything.

"You're right. I won't call Gabriela. Has Nick had any luck tracking down that guy that looks like Ed North?"

"He's still working on it."

Dana agreed to meet with Cheyenne in two hours at the bookstore slash cafe. She felt so powerless to help Benny.

Since Nick didn't seem to make headway with that facial-recognition stuff, Dana called her friend in Silicon Valley, Bucky Moreland.

Bucky had made a boatload of money as a software engineer for two Silicon Valley unicorn companies. He had been there from the early days of the startups and had become a multimillionaire in the process. Bucky was now one of those Silicon Valley ultra-high-net-worth techies who had retired and could toss money into projects he liked as an angel investor. Dana had met him at Stanford before he hit the big time. They'd stayed close, and he was her go-to person when she needed help with the tech stuff. He'd even programmed her bookstore's backend system just for fun.

"Hey, girl, what's up?"

"Hey, Bucky. I'm in a bit of pickle. I need your help."

"What's going on?"

Dana told him everything she knew.

"Hey, I'm sure it's just a mix-up and Benny will be fine," Bucky said, not sounding too reassuring.

"Listen, Bucky, I've been looking into a few things down here."

"Uh-oh, I know that tone in your voice, Dana. Don't bite off too much more than you can chew, especially being so far from home now, in another country, no less."

"I am home. And you know me, I'm cool as a cucumber."

They actually laughed about that, since she was usually wound pretty tight. It was the first time Dana had laughed in hours, and it felt nice.

"There was this creeper that was hanging around my bookstore right before all heck broke loose. And I don't know if he is mixed up in this whole mess, but... Are you familiar with facial-recognition software?"

"You kidding me? Of course. I have access to a primo face-searching tool. One of the best in the planet."

"So if I send the video footage of this guy, you could use that tool to find him?"

"I can try. Send it to me. But couple warnings. I can't guarantee we get a hit. And the process might take some time, since I'll be scanning a huge database that has more than a billion images."

"That's okay, maybe we'll get lucky."

Dana thanked her friend and then she emailed him the video. She knew it was a long shot, but at least she felt she was doing something to help Benny. But she wasn't done yet. She wasn't one to sit around twirling her thumbs, waiting for Bucky's software to scan a billion images. She had to figure out what the heck was going on. Cheyenne's words hung heavy in her mind: *You haven't known him that long, have you?*

Back at Cheyenne's rental house, she was sitting on the patio, putting the final touches on the script for the podcast. It was surreal to work, surrounded by the beauty of a tropical forest within a stone's throw from the Pacific Ocean. She looked over the script and sighed loud enough for Nick to hear it. He popped out of the house from the patio door. "I heard that. Are you stuck on the script?"

"No, it's not that. It's actually coming along nicely. The words are just pouring out of me."

"That's good. So why the long face?"

"I like Dana and feel bad about how this is panning out for her."

"It's kind of panning out worse for her boyfriend. He's the one in jail," Nick said.

"If he's guilty, then he made his own bed, so he'll have to lie in it. But this is all coming out of left field for Dana."

"I can't imagine finding out the person you love is a killer," Nick said.

"Let's not jump the gun, Nick."

Nick looked at Cheyenne, confused. "I've read the other scripts you've finished writing. You make a compelling case that Benny killed Terri because she was going to expose him as the perpetrator of Ed North's death."

"I'm just the storyteller, and I tell the story how it unfolds. But it doesn't make it easy when my podcast is going to inflict a world of hurt on someone I like." Cheyenne became teary-eyed at the thought. It was the hard part of her job.

"It won't be our first rodeo in that department. We're always going to have people upset or hurt in our line of work. It's just the way it is," Nick said rather coldly. But Cheyenne knew he was telling the truth.

"I know that. But it doesn't make it any easier."

Nick walked over to a red cooler. "What you need right now is a delicious, soothing agua de pipa. Nectar from the heavens, right out of a coconut shell. It's soul cleansing."

Nick opened the cooler. He had it packed to the gills with ice. He dug out two coconut shells from the dozen he had bought from a roadside vendor. In Costa Rica, coconuts grew like crazy, especially on the beach. The locals called a coconut "pipa." Thus *agua de pipa*—coconut water. Agua de pipa was best served cold. And the best, more natural way to do that was just chill the whole coconut in ice.

Nick put the two shells on the ground and used a machete he had bought at the market to cut off an opening in the top of one of the shells. He then dropped a straw into the shell and handed it to Cheyenne.

"Thanks. You're getting pretty handy with that machete," Cheyenne said, taking a drink.

It tasted so good and refreshing. But it didn't change how terrible she felt inside. The next teaser episode of the podcast was going to drop tomorrow, and she felt like she was backstabbing Dana.

Chapter Sixteen

DANA BEGAN the day by going over a treasure trove of public records regarding Terri and Burt Kaminski from the United States. She had purchased several legal documents online. It boggled the mind how much information could easily be purchased on a person online for less than fifty dollars. She could map out a sordid and messy legal trail that was the life of the late Terri Kaminski.

Theresa Mancuso's childhood had been tough. Her father had been arrested on many occasions on domestic violence charges. He abandoned Terri and her mother and two brothers when Terri was twelve. Dana knew from other interviews with Terri after Ed's disappearance made news that she ran away from home when she was seventeen. She was arrested a few times for petty crimes: passing bad checks, trespassing, dine and dashing, and theft. Dana was surprised to learn that Terri had grown up hard on the streets. No wonder she acted hard. It wasn't an act; it was her survival instinct. She grew up having to scratch and claw to survive. She married at eighteen, but the marriage didn't last a year. Soon after that she met Ed North, and three months later she was Terri North.

In ten years of marriage to Ed North, she reinvented herself as a rich-housewife-of-Miami type. Ed disappeared, and she took on Ed's first family—his ex-wife and their children—tooth and nail over Ed's vast estate. The controversial last will that Terri claimed to have found in Ed's safe left everything to her and nothing to his children. Lawsuits from Ed's kids began flying soon after the disputed will turned up. She declared Ed presumed dead on the first day she could do so under Florida law, much to the North kids' chagrin.

On the second day of Ed being declared legally dead, she married Burt Kaminski. In the seven years since Ed vanished, there had been many legal battles between the North kids and Terri. She had beaten them in court time after time. Ed's fortune had become her fortune. And now she was dead. All that money, all that fighting. And for what? The one time she met Terri at the bookstore, Dana saw an embittered pit viper ready to strike out at everyone.

Mild-mannered as he seemed to be, Burt Kaminski also had some legal shenanigans in his past, which surprised Dana. Burt had done a couple of years in prison on two different stints. Dana was amazed. Wow. You just never know about people's past when you meet them in their present incarnation.

Even though the Kaminskis had gone through a bevy of legal entanglements during their lifetime, nothing really screamed out that Terri could kill Ed and do it so well that she got off scot-free without the body ever being discovered. There were rumors she dumped the body in the Florida everglades, where the gators devoured the evidence on her behalf. But most of the rumors came from the North family and Ed's former business partners who were cut off from Ed's millions, all thanks to Terri. If anyone had motive to kill Terri, it would be the North kids, who were close in age to their former stepmother. Dana looked at the image of the creeper Ed North-lookalike. "Or maybe you're still alive, you slick troublemaker," Dana said out loud to Wally.

She wondered how Bucky's creeper search was going when her phone rang. It was Bucky.

"We got lucky," Bucky said.

"You got a hit?" Dana said, getting excited. She felt a flutter of butterflies in her stomach.

"I ran a query on my server last night and boom, we have a match. And only five hours later. Someone up there likes you, girl."

"Oh my gosh, Bucky, thank you! So? Who is he?"

"He's not Ed North. His name is Paul Glabb. He's a Florida-based actor. Do you know him?"

"Never heard of the guy. An actor?"

"That's why we got a hit so quickly. He has his acting headshot photographs plastered all over the internet. We got a match off his profile in a website called *First Call*."

"What kind of site is that?"

"It's a job-searching website for actors. If you're looking to hire an actor, you go to their website to enter the type of actor you're looking for, and then you can look through the large database of actors," Bucky explained. "Sorry, kid, I know you hoped that was Ed North, but it's just an actor, probably on vacation down there in Costa Rica."

Dana looked at the still image of the video feed of the creeper she now knew as Paul Glabb. She put the picture of Ed North next to the actor's. The resemblance was uncanny.

"Seems like a heck of a coincidence," Dana said.

"What do you mean?"

"This Paul Glabb is the spitting image of Ed North. Heck, he's even dressed like Ed North on my video security footage. And he's hanging around here like he wants to be seen. And you said he's an actor from Florida, which is where Terri and Burt

Kaminski live. What are the odds, Paul Glabb? Professional actor. Who just so looks just like Ed North. Suddenly shows up and comes to Mariposa Beach. We're a bit off the beaten path. And he's here at the same time Terri and Burt are in Costa Rica. That's all too much for it to be mere happenstance."

"Sometimes odd coincidences are just that. Odd coincidences," Bucky said.

Dana pulled up Paul Glabb's profile from the *First Call* website. There were about a dozen photographs of him. Headshots. Action shots. Glabb looking pensive. Another one of him looking scared. A headshot of him in a suit, smiling wide. Even when he was dressed up differently, the resemblance to Ed North was there.

A similar haircut and clothing to Ed North's would be all it took if someone wanted to trick Dana and Cheyenne into thinking Ed was still alive.

But why? Dana wondered.

"I wonder whether there is a way to find out if Paul Glabb is still in the country."

"That's above my skill set without hacking into Costa Rica's customs website or something," Bucky said.

"Yeah, that's a bit extreme. But I know someone who just might help without breaking hacking laws."

Dana thanked Bucky and immediately called Cheyenne.

Back at her Airbnb, Cheyenne hung up the phone with Dana.

"What was all that about?" Nick Suárez asked, having overheard Cheyenne's one-sided conversation.

"Dana came across something very interesting," Cheyenne said slowly, processing the newfound information.

"Do tell?"

"Remember that creeper in the video that looks like Ed North?"

"Yes, of course. Sorry, but I've come up with goose eggs trying to rule him out as not being Ed North," Nick said.

"Don't worry about that. Dana found him."

"She did? How?"

"She's from the Bay Area, so one of her friends is one of those tech millionaire geniuses with too much time in his hands and Dana sent him the video. He used his own facial-recognition software and got a match."

"So soon? I'm impressed. I assume our mystery man isn't Ed North."

"No. His name is Paul Glabb."

"Paul Glabb?"

"That's right. He's a Florida-based actor. Quite the coinky-dink. Don't you think?"

"I don't know. Many people come to Costa Rica from all over the US to hit the beaches," Nick said.

"Ed North's doppelgänger is right here in Mariposa Beach. At the same that we're here to produce our podcast. And at the same time as Terri Kaminski. That doesn't jive well with me," Cheyenne said.

"Okay, so it doesn't pass the smell test. What are you going to do?"

"Dana wanted me to reach out to my police source to see if our actor friend Paul Glabb really came to Costa Rica and if he's still in the country."

Chapter Seventeen

DANA WAS FEELING MORE positive about her little amateurish investigation. She had Cheyenne looking into Paul Glabb. And she had uncovered a lot of interesting background information on Terri and Burt. Terri had inherited all of Ed's money. Burt didn't have any tangible assets or money that she could find in his name. He had stopped working his sales jobs after marrying the former Terri North. Perhaps that's why he seemed to walk on eggshells around her. She was his sugar mamma, and he didn't want to upset the applecart.

The phone rang, startling Dana from her thoughts. It was Benny's lawyer, Shirley Pacheco. She picked up the call.

"Hi Dana, I'm afraid I have some bad news."

Dana's heart sank.

"The judge granted the prosecutor's request to hold Benny under preventive detention. It's hard to argue against it when the murder weapon was found in Benny's safe. Sorry. I have failed to get him out of jail. But I'm not done fighting yet."

"Have they determined that it was the murder weapon for sure?"

"The lab is testing the blood and hair they recovered off the tire iron, so hopefully we'll know in a few days. But it doesn't look good, Dana."

"How's he doing? Will I be able to talk to him or visit him?"

"He's holding up, all things considered. I've ensured he stays in the holding cell of the OIJ headquarters in San José, which is like the Hilton compared to the San Leon preventive prison where they wanted to transfer him."

"I've heard about that place. It's the type of prison right out of *Locked Up Abroad*. One's worst nightmare."

"It's an overcrowded, hot mess, and I'm working hard to get him released before he's transferred to that forsaken place," Pacheco said.

"Thank you."

"As for visiting him. You should be able to visit in about forty-eight hours, since he's now been processed under that court order versus the twenty-four-hour hold, and this country loves its bureaucratic paperwork to make that happen. I'll be heading down to Mariposa Beach tomorrow. Can you meet me at Benny's place at noon?"

"Yes, of course. Do you need a ride or are you driving?"

"I'm on the first flight out there on Tropic Air. My assistant rented a car, so we're all set, thank you."

As terrible as she felt over the dreadful news about Benny, Dana couldn't help but smile thinking of this high-powered, take-no-prisoners attorney sitting in one of Captain Junior's puddle-jumper planes on the way to Mariposa Beach from the capital. But it made sense; as bumpy as that plane ride was, it saved like five hours in traffic that could be just as scary as the turbulent flight down through the mountains over the tropical forests and onto the Guanacaste coast.

After getting off the phone with Shirley Pacheco, Dana felt hungry. There wasn't much she could do, so she went to the Qué Vista Restaurant to get a bite to eat on the beach and clear her head, get out of the house where she had been cooped up, scrunched over her laptop, since yesterday.

She grabbed her keys and climbed into Big Red.

The restaurant's owner, María Rivera, greeted Dana warmly. Right away, she noticed the group of septuagenarian and octogenarian ladies known as the Gossip Brigade having tea and sandwiches while playing canasta. Rumors spread like wildfire when the old biddies got together. Doña Chilla was the youngest member of the group—the baby, as the other members had nicknamed her—having just turned seventy-nine years old. She waved Dana over.

"Crud," Dana said under her breath. María heard her and smiled at Dana.

"You thought you could dodge that bullet, huh?"

"It had crossed my mind," Dana said, heading over to Gossip Brigade's table.

"Good afternoon, ladies. Who's winning?"

"That would be me," Doña Marta said, wiggling her fingers in the air at Dana.

"Only because you're cheating," Doña Amada, the curmudgeon and de facto leader of the group, sneered.

"I'm not cheating. You're just a sore loser," Doña Marta protested.

"Ladies, please," María said, trying to diffuse another argument.

"We're so sorry to hear about Benny. How's he doing, dear?" Doña Chilla said. She was just as nosey as the rest of the brigade, but she had a sweet demeanor about her, especially compared against the rough-around-the-edges bluntness of Doña Amada.

Dana looked at María and could see in her embarrassed facial expression that she knew. If the Gossip Brigade knew Benny had been arrested, the news was certainly spreading through town. Soon it would start making its way through the other small beach-town communities. Stopping gossip in a small town was like trying to stop water from gushing out by putting your finger in the hole of a dam.

"What happened to Benny?" Doña Luz asked. Dana didn't know if she was being coy or her eighty-year-old mind was misfiring a bit that day.

"The police arrested him for killing that woman up in the resort," Doña Amada said. Her tone was matter-of-fact, and she hardly looked up from her hand of cards, seemingly more concerned about her next hand than what was happening to Benny.

Dana wanted to protest and tell her how wrong she was, and that she shouldn't be spreading such vile rumors. But...she wasn't lying. That's why Benny was in jail. Under suspicion of murder. Dana was losing her appetite.

"Oh, rubbish, Benny couldn't hurt a fly," Doña Luz said.

Dana offered her a thin smile.

"Is he all right, honey?" Doña Chilla asked her.

"He's doing well, all things considered. His lawyer will be in town tomorrow, and soon the truth will come out and Benny will be back here before you know it," Dana said. She hoped they couldn't see through the effort she was going through to stand there, pretending that everything was going to work out.

Doña Amada guffawed at what Dana said.

"Anyway. Are we going to play cards or not?" she complained.

"I'll leave you ladies to your game," Dana said, walking away. She could hear Doña Luz chiding Doña Amada. "Why do you have to be so mean to the poor girl?"

"What? I just said what I heard. The truth stinks sometimes. Don't get mad at me," Doña Amada said, her voice gloriously fading away the farther Dana walked.

"Sorry about that, Dana. You know how Doña Amada is. No filter," María said.

"It's okay. I'm used to her ways by now."

María sat Dana at one of the tables on the beach, which was as far as she could get away from the Gossip Brigade without going into the ocean.

"Is this far away enough from the Brigade?"

"Perfect," Dana said with a smile.

She ordered her usual shrimp and rice, which came with a lovely side salad consisting of lettuce and palmito—palm heart— and fried yuca. The sand was hard and wet from the afternoon downpour. But it was lovely out. She looked out at the waves lazily coming ashore and then receding back out to sea.

She felt sad, being out for dinner without Benny. She wondered how he was doing in the cold and hard cell one hundred and fifty miles away from her.

After dinner, Dana climbed into Big Red and fired her up. She exited the parking lot and headed home. It was a quick drive down Main Street, past Ark Row to the turnoff into the rutted dirt road that led up to Casa Verde. Her mind was racing with everything that was going on. She was hoping to hear from Cheyenne soon about Paul Glabb. And she was looking forward to meeting with Benny's lawyer the next day so she could really help Benny out of this mess.

Dana zoomed down Main Street. She pumped her brakes to make the turnoff up to her place when, to her horror, the brake pedal went straight down to the floorboard. *That's odd*, she thought, not thinking much about it. She tried again and again, and each time the pedal went straight down to the floorboard. Big Red wasn't slowing down. It was going faster. Panic mode kicked in as Dana grabbed the steering wheel with both hands as she frantically pressed on the brake pedal to no avail. She looked like Fred Flintstone trying to stop the Flintmobile with his bare feet to the ground.

"Oh my Lord," she screamed as Big Red picked up speed. She felt the Jeep getting more and more out of control.

There were a few people walking alongside the road, so she blared the horn, shouting, "Get out of the way. No brakes."

She turned the wheel and felt as Big Red fishtailed. Dana looked up in a panic and saw she was careening out of control into the biggest palm tree in Mariposa Beach. *This is not going to be good*, she thought as she closed her eyes and braced for impact.

Chapter Eighteen

WARM SALT WATER flooded into Big Red. Dana could feel her feet warm and wet and suddenly the water was up to her chest. She looked around. It was surreal. She was in the Pacific Ocean, which had stopped the runaway Jeep. And she was alive and in one piece. Dana was still in shock, but her adrenaline was pumping as she unbuckled her seatbelt and climbed out of Big Red into the ocean. She turned to swim away from the sinking Jeep. She saw Leo Salas and a couple of tourists running into the water after her. Leo was a fast swimmer, and he got to Dana first.

"I got you," Leo said, grabbing a hold of Dana's arm. Dana looked up to see her beloved Big Red waddling in the water. She cried, glad to be alive but horrified about losing Big Red to the mighty Pacific. She loved that Jeep, which she had inherited from her uncle. He had refurbished it and it had been his pride and joy for thirty years. In one year of Dana owning it, she had sunk it.

As she sat on the beach in shock, she saw Big Mike and Carlitos Moreno, who worked for Big Mike at his surf shop, come out of nowhere on a pair of WaveRunners. Big Mike flashed Dana a big smile and a hang-five hand salute at her as he shouted, "Don't worry, we won't let Big Red sink."

Mindy and Amalfi soon joined Dana, wrapping a towel around her as they tried to comfort her.

"What happened?" Mindy asked.

"My brakes gave out while I was driving home from Qué Vista. I was about to hit that enormous palm tree on Main Street. I just closed my eyes, waiting for impact, but then a little voice inside yelled at me: Are you nuts? You're going to die hitting that tree head on at this speed, so open your darn eyes now. So I did, just in time for me to yank the steering wheel. Big Red almost flipped, but I was able to correct and change course away from the tree and I just aimed for the open water."

"My goodness, that was smart thinking," Mindy said.

"Next thing I know, I'm in the water inside the Jeep, so I got out and Leo was there to help me swim back to shore," Dana said. She turned toward Leo, who was crouched behind her on the sand, soaking wet. "Thank you so much, Leo."

"Don't sweat it. I just saw Big Red tearing across town toward the water. I know you like to drive pretty fast and crazy, but that seemed way off, even for your driving," Leo said with a grin.

Dana managed a smile. She felt the shock wearing off and the adrenaline dump hit her hard. As she tried to stand up, her legs wobbled. She watched as Big Mike and Carlitos hooked up Big Red to their ropes, which they used for tow-in surfing. They revved the WaveRunner's engines and slowly towed the Jeep to shore where they were able to get Big Red's tires to hit the sand. José Luis, the unofficial parking lot security guard for Ark Row, opened the driver's side door as water gushed out from Big Red. He hopped inside and steered as Big Mike and Carlitos pulled it back onto the beach shoreline and onto solid ground. Jose Luis tried turning the ignition, but it was toast.

He looked at Dana. "Sorry, Doña Dana. Such a beautiful Jeep."

"Thanks, José Luis."

Dana turned around and noticed that just about the entire town of Mariposa Beach was standing either on the sidewalk overlooking the beach or right on the beach, watching the spectacle. She could see the Gossip Brigade from the sidewalk gawking, shaking heads, and pointing. *How embarrassing*, Dana thought. She wanted to run back into the water and hide.

"So odd that the brakes would go out like that," Leo said, looking at the Jeep-turned-boat that was Big Red.

"Moisés takes excellent care of Big Red. He just worked on her a couple of weeks ago. She was in tiptop shape," Dana said.

Dana stood there, figuring out what to do with Big Red. She just wanted to go home and rest. The crowd of onlookers seemed to refuse to dissipate. The locals and even the tourists whom she didn't know kept asking her if she was all right and what had happened. She thanked everyone again for their help and their concerns for her wellbeing.

"I'm fine. Really. I just want to go home."

Big Mike drove his big Toyota Tundra right onto the beach. He hooked up Big Red to a tow strap. "We're ready to rock 'n' roll, Dana," Big Mike said.

Dana hugged Mindy and Amalfi, saving the biggest hug for Leo. Then she climbed into the passenger seat of Big Mike's truck and he got her and Big Red back home.

"Thank you so much for everything, Big Mike," Dana said.

"No worries, D, you know we all got each other's back out here in our little beach community."

Dana could feel tears streaming down her cheeks.

"Hey there, you're good. I know you love Big Red, but that's just stuff, man. You're safe and sound, and that's what's important."

Dana hadn't seen this Zen-like side of Big Mike, whose real name was Mike Pavlopoulos. He was short and scrawny, which begged the question of his nickname, Big Mike. It wasn't because of his physical attributes but because of his big-wave surfing past. He was like a forty-year-old version of Jeff Spicoli, even though he was born and raised in landlocked Kansas not in Southern California.

"I know this has been a bummer, but man, Dana, that was gnarly, how you maneuvered that out-of-control Jeep without brakes across town right into the water. It was totally awesome. But sorry about your Jeep. That stinks, bro."

All Dana could do was crack up.

"No worries, Big Mike; thanks again for all your help."

"You're going to be okay alone?"

Dana turned to see Ramón and Carmen jogging up toward them with worried looks on their faces.

"I'm not alone," Dana said with a smile.

Chapter Nineteen

ONCE INSIDE HER HOUSE, Dana crumbled. The shock of what had happened finally settled in her head and it hit her like a ton of bricks. Wally gave her a silent meow that melted her heart. She picked him up, and although he didn't like being manhandled for too long, he let Dana cuddle him for as long as she needed without flipping out. It was like Wally sensed she was feeling distraught.

"You're a little empath, aren't you, kitty?" Dana said. She put Wally down, went to the kitchen and made some tea to calm her nerves.

Her phone rang. She looked at the caller ID. It was Freddy Sánchez, a police officer with the Tourist Police Unit in Playa Guiones. Mariposa Beach didn't have a police presence in town. The closest substation was in Playa Guiones, which was about ten miles away. Officers from that substation made the rounds up and down the coast, patrolling the beach communities like Mariposa Beach on motocross motorcycles. The bikes were made for off-road riding, so they were an ideal way to get around quickly and without trouble on dirt roads or on the sandy beaches.

"Hey, Freddy."

"Hi, Doña Dana. A call came through about your accident. I'm on my way," Freddy said.

"Okay, thank you."

"Please make sure no one touches the vehicle, okay?"

"Sure, Freddy."

Dana hung up. All she wanted to do was soak in her bathtub for like an hour, but that would have to wait. She walked outside. Ramón was inspecting the Jeep.

"Ramón, Freddy Sánchez just called me. He's on his way. He asked that we don't mess with the Jeep. So better stay clear until he arrives."

"Yes, of course," Ramón said, backing away from the Jeep as if it were radioactive.

Fifteen minutes later, Officer Freddy Sánchez arrived. He climbed off his motorcycle and removed the helmet. He wore the uniform of the tourism police's unit: a white short-sleeve polo shirt with blue collars. They embroidered the patches of the National Police Force and the Tourist Division into the chest area of the shirt. One patch on the left, the other on the right. Blue khaki pants with a radio clipped on the side and a Glock pistol in its holster completed the uniform.

Freddy removed a black baseball hat from his pocket and put it on. It had the word POLICÍA—POLICE—emblazoned in large yellow letters on the front panel of the hat.

"Are you okay, Doña Dana?" Freddy asked.

"I'm fine, just shaken up."

Freddy turned his attention to Big Red, and he seemed crestfallen to see the vintage Jeep in such a condition.

"So what happened?"

Dana told Freddy everything that went down. How she left the restaurant on her way home but her brakes failed, so she drove into the ocean to stop the out-of-control vehicle before it hit a building, tree, or even worse, a person.

"That was the smart play," Freddy said. He walked around the Jeep, taking photographs of it with his smartphone. "Have you been having mechanical problems recently?"

"None. She was in tiptop shape. Moisés just changed the oil and inspected everything a few weeks ago. And he's good at his job," Dana said.

Freddy nodded in agreement. "I know Moisés well." Dana smiled. Everybody knew everybody in these parts. "He's a darn good mechanic."

Freddy took some more pictures of the Jeep before getting down on his knees and looking underneath it. He seemed to reach for something. He got back to his feet, looking at his hand, which was all greasy.

"What's that?"

"Brake fluid," Freddy said as he popped the hood and looked at the motor. He wiped his hands on his pant leg. He gave Dana a concerned look, then began taking pictures of the engine with his phone.

"Can you tell what happened?" Dana asked after he had taken about a dozen pictures.

"Looks like the brake line was cut," Freddy said ominously.

"Cut? Like it snapped or something?"

"I'm not an expert, but it looks to me like someone cut it with a knife. But the CSI team will be in charge of making that call official," Freddy said as he tapped on his phone's keys.

"Cut?" Dana said in an almost whisper. She slowly walked toward Big Red and stood there in disbelief. She heard Freddy calling in the OIJ, who would conduct the actual investigation.

He hung up. "It's going to be a while before they get here," he said.

Freddy went to the saddleback pouch on his motorcycle and he removed yellow police tape.

"You're going to put that crime scene tape around my Jeep?" Dana said.

"It's just to secure the vehicle, make sure it's not touched by anyone. Unfortunately, that includes you, Doña Dana. You can't access your vehicle until the OIJ arrives to investigate."

Dana couldn't believe what was going on. But she knew Freddy was just doing his job.

"Do you know anyone that would do this?" Freddy asked.

"To cut my brake line so I crash my car? No. I can't imagine anyone would do this on purpose," Dana said, her voice cracking as she realized what might have just gone down.

Was someone trying to kill her?

"Any arguments? A road rage incident? Anything you can think of?" Freddy asked. Dana knew he was asking questions above his pay grade. The only police entity that could conduct a criminal investigation was the OIJ. She wasn't going to get into the whole brouhaha with the recently departed Terri Kaminski and how her whole life began to unravel the moment that Cheyenne Lively decided to make Ed North the subject of her next podcast. And the irony of how she was one of Cheyenne's so-called true crime fiends. It wasn't much fun when the true part of true crime involved her real life—Dana's friends, Benny, her small beach-town community. It seemed her small corner of this tropical paradise had been turned upside down with a nefarious element ever since Cheyenne and Terri came to town.

"That darn podcast," Dana seethed.

"What podcast?" Freddy asked.

Dana didn't realize she had said that out loud.

"Oh, it's this true crime podcast called *What Really*

Happened. They're doing a story on the disappearance of Ed North."

"I remember that. It was big news around here for many years."

"It's going to be big news again with this podcast covering the story. I've been helping the podcaster, Cheyenne Lively, with it. And I'm thinking that someone out there really doesn't want that podcast to air," Dana said, looking around, feeling as if she were being watched. She looked at Big Red, which had been cordoned off by Freddy's yellow police tape. Surreal.

Chapter Twenty

OVER THE NEXT FEW HOURS, Casa Verde became as busy as Grand Central Station. Freddy Sánchez stood watch over Big Red. Moisés Conejo, Dana's mechanic, stopped by. Word was out about what had happened to Dana and to Big Red. He apologized. Dana reassured him he had absolutely nothing to apologize for, since the police believed the brake line was cut intentionally.

Moisés wanted to inspect Big Red, but Freddy wouldn't allow it until the OIJ conducted their investigation and released the Jeep back to Dana. A frustrated Moisés left.

Then Cheyenne Lively and Nick Suárez arrived.

"Are you okay?" Cheyenne asked Dana.

"I'm fine. My poor Jeep took the brunt of the abuse. I'm just feeling a little shaken up."

"A little? You're tough as nails. I heard you drove the Jeep with no brakes through town, avoiding people, trees, and buildings as you went into the water."

"Good gravy. How did you get the entire play-by-play?"

Cheyenne laughed. "You know how it goes in a small town. Everyone is talking about your adventure."

"Oh, wonderful."

"I grew up in a small town in Nebraska, remember? So I know what it's like when the entire town is into your business. I guess even though this is a different country, the rules of small-town living and gossiping still apply."

"It's quite different from living in a big city like San Francisco, where people hardly look up from their phones. And you develop that off-to-the-distance stare so no one messes with you," Dana said.

"It's how it is in L.A. too," Cheyenne said.

"Do you miss it?"

"Los Angeles?"

"No. Living in a small town."

Cheyenne thought about Dana's question for a moment.

"I miss the peace and quiet. And I miss the familial closeness in those types of rural communities. But I don't miss living in Nebraska. It was a great place to grow up, but I wanted to see more of the world. Like right now, being here in Costa Rica. Do you miss city living in San Francisco?"

"The only thing I really miss is having so many choices of great places to eat—Mexican, Chinese, Japanese, Filipino, Italian, a greasy burger, or some fancy fusion dinner. You can find it all in San Francisco. Oh, and I also miss Karl the Fog, since it's so hot down here all the time," Dana said with a smile.

Cheyenne looked out the window toward Freddy and the taped-up crime scene.

"This is crazy. You think this has anything to do with this whole Terri and Ed mess?" Cheyenne asked.

"Seems so. Things started getting strange and dangerous since you guys got to town for the podcast," Dana said. She didn't mean to sound accusatory. It was a simple fact.

"We usually run into anger and pushback when we work on

these cases, but nothing to this level. Terri is dead. And now looks like someone tried to kill you."

That was something Dana didn't want to consider, but it was an idea that had crept into her head. Hearing Cheyenne say it out loud made her really think about it, and it scared her. Was someone really trying to kill her, and why?

"No offense, but if someone wanted to stop your reporting and the podcast, why didn't they cut your brakes instead of mine?"

"Good point." Cheyenne turned toward Nick. "We'll have to check our car before we drive it anywhere."

Nick looked horrified. "Yeah, this is getting a little hairy. I'm a podcast producer. It's not like we're reporting in a combat zone," Nick said. He also looked out the window toward Big Red sitting behind yellow tape. Officer Freddy was sitting on a folding chair Dana had brought out for him. Nick shrugged his shoulder. "Maybe the network can send us some security. I thought they had Terri's killer locked up, but now, I don't know."

Dana glared at Nick, knowing he was talking about Benny.

"Sorry," Nick said sheepishly, looking down at the ground.

Cheyenne changed the subject. "Do you have any other enemies? Maybe this has nothing to do with Ed North, Terri, or the podcast."

"Do I have enemies that would want to cut my brake line so I would crash my Jeep and die? No. I do not."

"Just looking at all the possibilities here," Cheyenne said, sounding defensive.

Just then, the front gate buzzer went off, easing the tension between Dana, Cheyenne, and Nick.

"That must be the OIJ," Dana said.

Dana let them in. She saw the white unmarked sedan of the OIJ. Gabriela Rojas was behind the wheel, waving. Jorge Picado was in the passenger seat, looking straight ahead. Two other vehicles were behind the sedan. *What the heck,* Dana thought.

"The cavalry has arrived," Cheyenne said, looking at the caravan of vehicles making its way up the long driveway. The sound of gravel crunching and motors running got louder as they approached. Behind Picado and Rojas's sedan was a double-cab white pickup truck with OIJ emblazoned on its side; following it was a tow truck, and bringing up the rear was another white pickup truck with Policía Fuerza Publica emblazoned on its side. They were the uniformed National Police that oversaw Freddy Sánchez's Tourist Police Unit.

"What are they all doing here?" Dana asked. She felt like in a trance.

"I guess they're taking this seriously. As they should," Cheyenne said.

"Oh snap, they're going to tow Big Red away, aren't they?" Dana said distraughtly, looking at the tow truck.

"Looks that way," Cheyenne said.

The police vehicles came to a stop as cops in uniform and in plainclothes piled out of them. Two uniformed cops walked up to where Officer Freddy had been sitting, but he was standing now. Three agents with blue jackets with OIJ emblazoned on the back began to inspect the Jeep. Picado and Rojas walked up toward Dana.

"How you doing? Did you get hurt?" Rojas asked.

"I'm fine, thank goodness. What's all this?"

"Officer Sánchez seems to believe that someone tampered with your vehicle. That's a serious crime. We take that very seriously," Picado said.

"Are you going to tow my Jeep?"

"Yes. It's not your Jeep now," Picado replied with the warmth of a snapping alligator.

"I beg your pardon?"

"That's a crime scene, now," Picado said pointing at Big Red.

Rojas stepped in, trying to diffuse the long-standing animosity between Dana and Picado.

"It's standard, Dana. You'll get it back once the CSI team finishes processing it."

"Where will they take it?"

"To the lab in Liberia. It's easier for the team to work there than out here in the elements. Especially during the rainy season," Rojas said.

"It's soaking wet," one of the OIJ agents out by the Jeep shouted over toward Picado, who turned and looked at Dana.

"You know I ended up in the ocean? It was the only way to stop the Jeep without crashing into something like a tree or a wall."

"I'm aware of what happened. I have Officer Sánchez's report. It will be a miracle if the forensics team can find any evidence of value in a vehicle that was submerged," Picado said, as if driving into the ocean were her first inclination.

"Sorry for the inconvenience," Dana said facetiously.

Picado ignored her, turning his attention to Cheyenne and Nick, who had been standing behind Dana. She had forgotten they had been there all along.

Picado glared at Dana and then at Cheyenne and Nick. "No press. You two out, now."

"They're not press, Inspector, they're podcasters," Dana said.

"It's okay. We don't want to be in the way. Let's go, Nick," Cheyenne said.

"Gladly," Nick said, almost running out toward the car.

"I'll call you later," Cheyenne said to Dana as she followed Nick out to their rental SUV.

After Cheyenne and Nick left, Picado took Dana's statement as the tow-truck operator hooked up Big Red to its rig. Thirty minutes later, Dana was all alone in the middle of her living room as she broke down in tears. A concerned Wally looked up at her, meowing.

It was late at night, and Dana had had enough of the rotten day. The only thing that brought her good thoughts was that she could finally take that soak in the bathtub. She drew an Epsom Salt–infused bath and lit two lavender candles. The candles were handmade by her yogi friend, Marisol Arias, who enjoyed making special energy-infused candles and soaps. Marisol claimed to have transferred universal energy through a Reiki process to her handmade soap bars. Dana wasn't sure about all that, but the soaps smelled divine, and they were chemical-free.

After a long bath, she toweled off and was putting on body lotion and face cream as Wally watched her like she was a weirdo.

"Don't judge me, you groom by licking yourself and spitting out hairballs, mister."

It was midnight, but she didn't feel ready for bed, so she made it to the lounge chair on the veranda with her Kindle Oasis and a mint tea. Dana looked into the darkness of the surrounding tropical forest, hearing the waves crashing down at the beach even though the sound reminded her of Big Red barreling into the water hours ago. The crashing waves soothed her. She shook off the bad memory. She didn't want to think about any of that tonight. It was so quiet and blissful that she wondered how such a place could bring so much heartache. She knew the answer to that: It wasn't the place; it was the human species. *But we're not all bad,* she thought as she remembered Leo coming to her rescue. Then Big Mike and Carlitos on their WaveRunner, saving Big Red from sinking. And Mindy and so many others on the beach worried about her, comforting her. There were bad apples out there cutting brake lines, but there were more people who were good, caring, and kind. And luckily, as bad as it seemed humans could be, there were more good than bad.

And as soon as she got a good night's sleep, she was going to find out who were the rotten apples behind all this chaos.

Chapter Twenty-One

DANA SLEPT IN. She woke up feeling rejuvenated. After a stretch, she went on one of her mind-clearing runs, taking off down the wooded trail leading from her property into town. She crossed Main Street, running onto the beach close to where Big Red had gone into the water. She cleared that memory from her head as she ran close to the shoreline. Her feet pounded the hard, wet sand, feeling the back splash from the breaking waves on her arms and face. Dana could almost hear a Vangelis synthesizer playing "Chariots of Fire" in her head as she ran out to the rock formation that signaled the end of the passable road between Mariposa Beach and the next beach community over, so she turned around and ran back home. Dana was out of breath when she got home—more than usual. *I shouldn't anger-run*, she thought with a smile.

She drank a glass of freshly squeezed orange juice in a couple of gulps, then fired up the coffee machine and took a shower. She got dressed to the smell of the beans being brewed. These were the beans from the farm of Leo's family, located in the highland coffee region of Terrazú. It was the best coffee

Dana had ever tasted, and she came from java-crazed San Francisco.

She was sipping coffee and making oatmeal for breakfast when her phone rang. She checked the caller ID: Benny Campos. Her heart stopped. She figured it was Benny's daughter, Beatrice, calling on his phone. She picked up the call and her heart melted when she heard Benny's voice.

"Surprise," Benny said.

"Oh my gosh, I can't believe it. They let you out?"

"I told you Shirley Pacheco was the best criminal lawyer in the country," Benny said.

Dana wished he were standing in front of her so she could hug and kiss him.

"I want to see you. I can leave here shortly," Dana said. Even though Big Red was out of commission, sitting somewhere at the OIJ station in Liberia, Dana had a Toyota RAV4 for longer trips, like up to the city.

"Not necessary. Shirley was planning to fly down this afternoon, so I'm catching a ride with her and I'll be in Mariposa Beach soon."

Dana felt excited.

"You've made my day; heck, my year."

"Shirley told me what happened to you with Big Red. I'm so sorry I wasn't there to help you these last few days when you needed me the most."

"No apology needed. Jeez, they locked you up," Dana said. "Besides, you would have just ended up in the water with me. Nothing you could have done once the brake pedal hit the floorboard."

"Still. I should have been there with you."

"Well, let's make sure we can put an end to all this nonsense with the police so you can go back to your normal life."

"We're working on that, believe me."

"Not to look a gift horse in the mouth, because I'm thrilled you're free, but why did they let you out?"

"Shirley used what happened to you as proof that there was someone else down there up to no good, and it wasn't me, since I was locked up. The judge gave the prosecutor twenty-four hours to actually charge me with a crime; if not, he would rescind the preventive-detention order. Shirley went to work, and the prosecutor conceded they needed more time, so they released me. I can't leave the country, but I'm free."

"Such wonderful news."

"This legal nightmare is far from over, but I'm seeing a light at the end of a gloomy tunnel."

Since Benny wouldn't be in Mariposa Beach until the afternoon, Dana got into her RAV4 and drove up to the Tranquil Bay Luxury Resort. It was the poshest resort in the area, and one of the most luxurious resorts on the coast. The resort was owned by Gustavo Barca, who was determined to buy the properties between the resort and the beach so his bon vivant guests could have exclusive access to the ocean without having to schlep through regular people's homes and businesses.

As Dana's property was one of those, she didn't much care for the egomaniacal developer's plans.

She pulled up to the front security checkpoint of the resort. She recognized the guard, Jimmy López. He waved her through. Dana kept expecting Gustavo Barca to ban her from his resort after a few run-ins over the land. She figured he adhered to the *keep your enemies close* mantra. She pulled into the fancy porte cochère of the resort.

"Did you put Big Red into storage for the rainy season?" the disappointed valet asked as he opened the door to the ho-hum dime-a-dozen RAV4. The valets loved parking Big Red.

"It's in the shop," Dana said. She left it at that, not wanting to get into that whole mess with the young valet.

She walked up to the front desk, where there were several staff members smiling widely as she approached.

"Doña Dana, welcome," a young woman said enthusiastically.

Dana didn't recognize the girl. She was beautiful. Dark olive skin. Her black hair pulled back. Brown, sparkly eyes. Expertly applied mascara and eyeliner, Cleopatra style.

"Hello," Dana said, looking at the name tag: Becky Morales. "Oh, you're Amalfi's friend. It's nice to meet you, finally," Dana said.

"Likewise." Becky smiled.

This was perfect, Dana thought. If anyone was going to help her in her last-minute harebrained idea to talk to Burt Kaminski, it was one of Amalfi's friends. Before she went to work for the bookstore, Amalfi worked at the resort. She hated the stuffiness of working for a luxury resort and having to cater to rich tourists. Gustavo Barca's insistence that hotel management be heavy-handed with its staff made it an unpleasant place to work for Amalfi, who was thrilled to jump ship and work at Bagels, Books, and Lattes.

"Can I help you with anything?" Becky asked.

"I was hoping to speak to Burt Kaminski. Is he still here?"

Becky nodded, then leaned over the counter to get closer to Dana.

"After his wife was killed, he changed rooms because he said it was too painful to stay in the same room, so he upgraded to the VIP villa."

Dana knew the layout of the resort pretty well; the VIP villas were the most luxurious of the luxury rooms available at the resort. The villas were actually like tiny houses nestled on the hillside, away from the main resort area. The mountains cradled each villa with stunning views of the ocean down below.

"Do you know how long he's staying for?"

Becky whispered even lower, "He said until his wife's killer is behind bars for good."

"Could you call him and tell him I would like to talk to him?"

Becky looked around nervously. "Hold on," she said, picking up the phone and putting it to her ear. "Good morning, Mr. Kaminski. This is Becky from the front desk. There is a Ms. Dana Kirkpatrick in the lobby here to see you. Yes, sir. That's right. Okay. I'll send over a driver right away. Yes, I'll let her know. Thank you, sir." Becky hung up and looked at Dana with a surprised expression. "He said he'll meet you in the Del Fuego Bar and Grill in about fifteen minutes. I'm going to have one of our service vehicles pick him up at his villa right away."

Dana took the wide and grand steps that led from the lobby down to the pool area. It was difficult not to get distracted and miss a step with the breathtaking views of the Pacific in front of her. The Del Fuego Bar and Grill was located right off the main pool—the resort had six pools and too many hot tubs to keep count. The grill was pretty empty at ten thirty in the morning. There was a man eating a burger and drinking a beer while reading a book. *A burger and beer, the breakfast of champions*, Dana thought as she sat at the table closest to the door.

A waiter was at her side before she had settled in. The service at the resort was well known for being meticulous. Dana found it stifling, like being besieged by pushy salespeople following you around the store.

"Good morning, ma'am. We don't serve breakfast at the Grill, but I'd be happy to bring you our regular lunch menu."

"I'm waiting for someone, so just coffee for now, please."

"Certainly, ma'am," the eager waiter said, scampering away to fetch her coffee.

Dana looked around at the grill and the pool area outside.

Then she turned her head up toward the main building, which sat perched above. It was a terrible thing to think, but if Gustavo Barca were drowning in the ocean, she'd sooner toss him a boulder than a life ring, but she had to hand it to him: He really knew how to build and run a swanky place like the Tranquil Bay Resort.

The waiter brought Dana her coffee. She thanked him as he scurried away again to who knows where. She took a sip, and the coffee was delicious. Ten minutes later, a small, white bubble-like vehicle pulled up to the side of the restaurant. It was one of those fancy golf carts used to transport guests around in these swanky resorts since walking must be just for the unwashed masses. Dana saw Burt hop out, and he made his way toward her.

"I must admit, this is quite the surprise, Ms. Kirkpatrick," Burt said. A wide smile was plastered on his tan face. His gray hair was combed back. He had thick hair, not bad for a man in his sixties. Dana picked up on a unique energy she hadn't noticed at her bookstore days earlier. Then, he seemed brow-beaten and henpecked standing next to the diminutive spitfire that was Terri. Now he seemed relaxed. Almost liberated. His attire had also changed. When she had first met him, he was dressed in a simple no-brand blue polo shirt and Dockers khaki pants, and now he was decked out in a pricey white silk Tommy Bahama shirt and Prada Bermuda shorts, with blue boat shoes on his sockless feet. *Someone hit one of the luxury shops at the resort*, Dana thought as she looked him over.

Burt sat down across from her as the waiter once again seemed to appear out of thin air. "I'll have a coffee and a mango juice," Burt ordered.

"I'm sorry for your loss, Mr. Kaminski," Dana said.

For a moment, it seemed as if Burt had forgotten he was a grieving spouse.

"Thank you. Very kind of you, Ms. Kirkpatrick."

"Please, call me Dana."

"Okay, Dana. Please call me Burt. Now, to what do I owe an out-of-the-blue visit like this?"

"I'm just trying to wrap my head around everything that's been going on here the last few days," Dana said.

"What do you mean?"

Dana's eyebrows furrowed. "You and Terri showing up here threatening lawsuits and shoving an NDA in my face at my place of business."

"I suggested to Terri that we let the lawyers handle all that, but when she got an idea in her head, it was hard talking her out of things. I suppose that's all water under the bridge now."

"How's that?"

"Terri is dead. Her killer has been caught. It probably won't be long until they get the evidence they need to charge him in Ed North's murder too," Burt said.

Dana tried to hold it together.

"Sorry. I know you're romantically involved with Benny Campos."

"No apologies needed because he's not guilty," Dana said.

The waiter dropped off Burt's coffee and mango juice. Burt took a big sip.

"Boy, they make a delicious juice. Do you want one? I recommend it," he said, as if they were pals enjoying each other's company.

"No thanks. Mr. Ka... Burt, I assure you Benny had nothing to do with your wife's murder."

"That's not what the police tell me."

"It's not the first time the police have been wrong in these matters."

"Touché. Let me tell you something, Dana. For seven years, Terri had to endure with the rumors and innuendos. The finger-pointing and staring. The whispering all over Miami that she killed her husband, and the viciousness of Ed's first wife and children. Angry and bitter because they were left with nothing in his will."

"Thanks to Terri trying to deflect that unwanted attention from herself, she did the same exact thing to Benny. Telling the Miami detectives that Ed came here to see Benny and that they were in some shady deals. So Benny has had to deal with the same scrutiny as your wife."

"Perhaps that's why he snapped and killed her," Burt said between sips of mango juice.

"That's not true."

"I suppose we can go back and forth all day. And for what? It's all in the authorities' hands now. Let them sort it out. And the podcast will cover it all as it unfolds, I suppose."

"You're not going to try to stop it?"

"Not now that they're onto the actual killer of Ed North and Terri."

Dana banged her fist on the table. "He's innocent."

"Sorry, Dana. I didn't mean to upset you."

"Someone tried to kill me yesterday. Tampered with my Jeep."

"The OIJ detectives talked to me about that, so I'm aware. I'm glad you're okay. Such a dastardly deed," Burt said.

"You wouldn't know anything about that?"

"Me? Heavens to Betsy, no. Besides, I'm not the handy mechanical type that would know how to cut a brake line."

"Does the name Paul Glabb mean anything to you?"

"No. Why do you ask?"

"He's an actor from Florida."

"I've never heard of him. What's he been in?"

"A private role to come to Mariposa Beach and hang around town, looking like Ed North."

"I beg your pardon?"

"Didn't you and Terri hire him to trick people into believing that Ed North was still alive?"

Burt laughed loudly.

"Oh, dear Dana, did you bump your head in that car crash?"

"Such a coincidence. You and Terri come here from Florida. This Florida-based actor that could be cast in the *Ed North Story* shows up at the same time."

Burt threw his hands in the air. "I don't have a clue what the heck you're talking about, to be honest."

"I think you do."

"What exactly are you expecting from me? Why did you come out here?"

"I want the truth."

"Like I said before, that's in the hands of the proper authorities now. So we'll just let them do their job, okay?" Burt said, getting up. He looked at the waiter, who was coming over. "Roberto, charge this to my room, please."

"Yes, sir. Mr. Kaminski."

"You should really try the mango juice. It's delicious," Burt said, walking away.

Dana sat there for a moment to gather herself before making more of a scene after slamming her fists on the table earlier. *Keep it together, girl*, she thought to herself.

Why did she come out here? Did she expect Burt to confess? And confess to what? Could he have killed Terri? And then tried to kill her? He seemed so mild-mannered. Why would he want Terri dead? But there was one thing for certain: Burt Kaminski didn't seem to be shedding too many tears over his wife's recent demise at the end of a steel tire iron.

Chapter Twenty-Two

DANA STOPPED at the bookstore on her way home from the resort. It was the dead zone between the morning breakfast and lunch crowds, so there was one customer walking out with a large cup of to-go coffee as Dana walked in. There was another customer sitting on one of the comfy reading chairs Dana had peppered around the store, enjoying a book, latte, and a bagel.

Amalfi was sitting at the sales counter. Dana wanted to make sure Amalfi was fine manning the bookstore on her own for the day.

"Sure, no problem," Amalfi said.

"I saw your friend Becky Morales up at the resort," Dana told Amalfi.

"I know, she texted me," Amalfi said sheepishly.

Jeez, there really is no privacy in a small community, Dana thought.

"What were you doing up there at the resort?" Mindy asked.

"I met up with Burt Kaminski."

"Why did you do that?" Mindy sounded concerned. Dana knew she made her friends—like Mindy here in Mariposa

Beach and her best friend, Courtney Lowe, back in San Francisco—worry about her. Courtney had once said that Dana gave her ulcers when she began meddling in these types of cases.

"I don't know. I just wanted to see what his deal was."

"The man just lost his wife, Dana," Mindy said.

"He didn't seem too grief-stricken to me."

"People grieve differently, especially in public."

"I expect you to burst out in tears several times a day for years when I'm gone," Leo told Mindy with a grin.

"Don't even say that, it's bad luck," Mindy said, making the sign of the cross.

"It was a waste of time, anyway. He seemed to revel in letting me know how the police arrested Benny for Terri's murder."

"I'm just glad he's out of jail," Mindy said.

"Me too," Dana said.

"When do you expect him?"

"In a few hours. So I'm going to go home and get ready. Make something good for dinner."

"It should be a wonderful reunion," Mindy said with a smile.

Dana got a lox bagel and coffee to go, and she headed home to prepare for Benny's arrival.

Dana barely had time to finish her lox bagel when her phone rang. It was Cheyenne.

"Great news about Benny. Why didn't you tell me they released him?"

"How the heck did you find out?"

"My police source."

"You're really connected there," Dana said. She felt a tinge of jealousy.

When she moved to Mariposa Beach, she toyed with the idea of starting one of those travel blogs and a podcast about moving to Costa Rica. Maybe write a book about it. But travel bloggers were a dime a dozen. It seemed there was a new blog or vlogger on YouTube popping up all the time, expounding on living the dream of ditching the fast-paced life in America for Costa Rica. So she decided to open a bookstore instead. It seemed a crazy idea to open a brick-and-mortar bookstore in the era of digital e-readers, but she did it anyway. She couldn't just hang out on the beach all day, retired at thirty-three. It sounds like fun until you're bored to tears.

"A birdy told me Benny is headed down to Mariposa Beach this afternoon," Cheyenne said.

"Nothing gets by you."

"Now is the time for Benny to talk to me. We can compare notes about the case. I really need his side of the story in all this for my podcast. And perhaps I can provide information to help him with his case."

Dana mulled it over. If anything, she wanted to see what dirt Cheyenne had over this sordid case. Following the lawyer playbook and saying nothing hadn't panned out well for Benny after all. He ended up spending almost three days locked up. It was time to take the bull by the horn rather than scurrying away from it, trying to hide.

"Why don't you come over at eight?"

Dana flew into Benny's arms the moment he walked through the door. "You look great," she marveled.

"I was only in the city lockup for three days. Not really hard time," Benny said with a grin.

"Where's Shirley? I wanted to thank her in person for getting you out."

"She's doing some work at my place with her investigator

and a paralegal. They're looking at my safe, trying to figure out how the killer accessed it to put that tire iron inside to frame me."

The safe was hidden in the floorboard in Benny's study, and he didn't announce that from the rooftops. So how could the killer have known to plant it there? And how did they open the locked safe? It's what Shirley Pacheco and her team were desperately trying to figure out.

"Who knew about the safe?" Dana asked.

"A couple of friends. My ex-wife. Beatrice. But no one knows the combination. That's what sealed my fate with Detective Picado. Not only would this mystery person have to know about the safe and its location, but then have the combination to open it and put the murder weapon inside."

"For now, I'm just so grateful that Shirley got you out of jail."

"She's great, but if we don't figure out who's behind all this right quick, I might end up back there, or even worse, at the actual penitentiary."

"We'll figure it out. But right now, let's eat. I made something special for you," Dana said, stepping into the kitchen.

She pulled out a large bowl from the fridge and put it on the kitchen counter. She removed the plastic wrap that was covering the dish.

"Yum, ceviche," Benny said.

Ceviche was a delicious seafood dish made from fresh raw fish that was cooked in lime juice.

"I used your secret ingredient to make it a Tico ceviche," Dana said with a smile. That secret ingredient was ginger ale. Benny scooped up ceviche into a saltine cracker, then splashed it with Lizano Tabasco sauce and washed it down with an ice-cold Imperial beer.

"Delicious. You made it like a local," he said with a smile.

For the main course, Dana brought out a bowl of arroz con pollo, which was one of Benny's favorite meals. Dana hadn't quite mastered making that Costa Rican dish, so she picked up a to-go order from the Qué Vista Restaurant.

"I cheated. It's from Qué Vista," Dana said.

"I appreciate the effort," Benny said, digging in.

After dinner, Dana checked the time. Cheyenne would arrive soon. All she wanted to do right now was just spend time with Benny on the couch, watching something silly on Netflix, but they needed to get to the bottom of this case before Benny ended up in prison or the killer tried to take another potshot at her.

"Benny, I've been talking with Cheyenne Lively, and I know she's just out for her own interest with the podcast, but she's an incredible journalist with sources in the police. She said she has information for us, so I told her to stop by tonight. Don't be mad."

"How could I get mad at you for trying to help me? I have nothing to lose hearing her out. Lord knows my ignoring her didn't pan out. I thought all this would just go away if I ignored it, but as usual, ignoring the problem just makes things worse."

A few minutes later, she got a text from Cheyenne. "She's on her way over," Dana told Benny. Then another text from Cheyenne:

Found our Ed North actor! Had chat will share when I get there. 10 minutes away.

Chapter Twenty-Three

CHEYENNE CAME ALONE. Dana showed her to the living room. Benny was standing a few feet away, seemingly unsure if it was the right thing to meet with the podcaster.

"It's great to finally meet you, Benny," Cheyenne said. Benny gave her a brief nod, but he said nothing, nor did he make any moves toward her, choosing to stand there with his arms crossed.

"Where's Nick?" Dana asked, eager to end the awkward meet between Cheyenne and Benny.

"He's back at the Airbnb, busy editing the podcast. It takes hours to edit a single episode."

Dana offered Cheyenne something to drink, but she declined. They sat in the living room, Dana and Benny taking the couch while Cheyenne occupied the matching loveseat. The tension was palpable, like being out on a first date that wasn't going well.

"You said on the phone that you found Paul Glabb?" Dana asked.

"I did. Tracked him down to a hotel near the airport in Liberia. We had an interesting chat."

"You talked to him?" Cheyenne's uncanny skill of getting people to talk to her amazed Dana. It worked on her, and now there was Benny, who had blocked her and had refused her many requests for an interview for months, although Cheyenne hadn't gotten him to crack yet.

"And just in the nick of time. He's on a seven a.m. flight to Florida tomorrow. He's very spooked after learning about Terri's murder," Cheyenne said.

Dana noticed both she and Cheyenne quickly glanced over at Benny. He must have felt all eyes on him, but he said nothing, nor did he react. He sat there, stoic. Benny's years of working as an attorney in tense negotiations and mediations were paying off, allowing him to master the art of not showing his hand emotionally when needed.

"So he knew her," Dana said.

"Terri and Burt hired him."

"Oh my gosh. What were they up to?"

"Paul didn't know. To him, this was just another acting gig. Terri contacted him through that casting website. She told him it was for a YouTube video. He just had to loiter around Main Street near your bookstore, looking like a stalker. Terri gave him the clothing he had to wear. Told him to dye his black hair sandy brown—just like Ed North's hair color. She even gave him the bottle of hair-coloring product to use. He didn't know that she was changing his appearance and giving him clothing to make him look like Ed North. He was just happy to have a paying acting gig that included an all-expenses-paid trip to Costa Rica."

"I don't understand. Why go through all that hassle?"

"To muck up the waters. Cause confusion," Benny said, speaking for the first time since Cheyenne's arrival.

"Bingo. Terri was intent on planting doubt to discredit the podcast," Cheyenne said.

"That has always been her MO. She didn't want Ed buying land out here, so she came up with all these crazy theories about why it wasn't a good idea. After he went missing, she was sure to throw me under the bus with her lies about my supposed shady dealings. Eager to plant that idea into the police's head versus actually finding what happened to Ed," Benny explained.

"She couldn't be responsible for Ed North's death if he's still alive, showing up in your video surveillance footage," Cheyenne said.

"Terri probably figured she would wait until Paul Glabb returned to Florida before playing her manipulation games with that video footage," Benny said.

"Making the connection to Paul Glabb would have been doubtful if not for your friend's facial-recognition software," Cheyenne said.

"Terri probably didn't know much about this type of technology available to tech-savvy private citizens like Bucky," Dana said.

"But once Terri was killed, Mr. Glabb got scared. Who can blame him? So he was hightailing it back to the States," Cheyenne said.

"What did Paul say about Burt? How involved was he in all this?"

"He only met him once. Burt spoke little. It was obvious to our actor buddy that Terri wore the pants in that relationship. But Burt knew Terri had hired the actor. So he knew what she was up to."

"Funny he hasn't mentioned that. At all," Dana said.

"I've tried to talk with Burt the last couple days, but he's not talking and he had me banned from the resort property," Cheyenne said.

"I talked with Burt this morning," Dana said.

"What?" Cheyenne and Benny said at the same time.

"I went up to the resort this morning and asked for him. He agreed to meet with me."

"Just like that?" Cheyenne said.

"Just like that," Dana replied. It felt good to her, finally having out-scooped the star journalist podcaster.

"How did that go?" Cheyenne asked.

Dana told them about her midmorning chat at the Del Fuego Grill. About his upgraded clothing attire and how he hadn't seemed to grieve too much over the loss of his wife.

"Amalfi's friend Becky works the front desk, and she told me that the day after Terri was killed, he moved from his suite to one of the VIP villas."

Benny whistled. "That's where the uber rich and the Hollywood famous stay. That will set him back around five thousand dollars per night."

"Becky said that he didn't want to stay in the room he shared with Terri after she was killed," Dana said.

"Grieve in even more luxury, I suppose," Cheyenne said.

"You don't think Burt is behind all this?" Dana asked.

"The surviving spouse in a murder was usually the prime suspect," Benny said.

"There isn't clear motive," Cheyenne said.

"With Terri out of the picture, Ed North's estate would be his alone," Benny said.

"I can look at the estate now that Terri is gone, but I'm assuming it all goes to him as the husband," Cheyenne said, jotting down a reminder in her notebook.

"Maybe it wasn't about the estate," Dana said.

"In my experience covering the crime beat for a decade, it's usually about the money. That even trumps the other big murder catalyst: love," Cheyenne said.

"Perhaps. But maybe he just got tired of being pushed around by Terri. I've seen enough episodes of *Snapped* to know that people can only take so much abuse before they snap," Dana said.

"How did that tire iron end up in Benny's safe, though?" Cheyenne asked.

"My lawyer and her team are working around the clock trying to figure that out," Benny said.

"My police source told me the tire iron was just a generic L-shaped one found in most vehicles' trunks, so that helped your case. It could have belonged to anyone."

"That's right. And when they impounded my Land Cruiser, they found my tire iron still in my truck, which also helped my case."

"Benny, I need to know. What was Ed North doing down here?" Cheyenne asked.

Benny looked at Dana, who nodded her approval of talking with Cheyenne about Ed.

"Nothing shady, I assure. I was less than three years out of law school, and it was my first year putting out my shingle to practice law solo. He was my first rich client. Not that you would know it from looking at him. He was shabbily dressed. Mild-mannered. I would learn later he was a self-made multi-millionaire. He started out owning a junkyard, which he turned into a premier ironwork shop in the Bronx, making curtain rods, towel rings, bars, hooks, and show curtain rings. Simple items, but made well. This was before they made all that stuff in China, so the business took off and he did very well for himself. He put some of his money into real estate investment. Started with a few fixer-upper homes, moved on to small apartment buildings, laundromats, and car washes. Went from being a junkyard scrapper eking out a living to becoming a multimil-lionaire."

"The American Dream," Cheyenne said.

"That's right. By the time I met him, he had sold his ironworks company for a small fortune and moved to Florida. He continued to be a real estate investor, increasing his net worth. He came off unassuming, a blue-collar kind of guy, but he was a shrewd businessman."

"He was already married to Terri when you met?"

"Yes. Not to talk ill of the dead, but I didn't care much for her. She was condescending. About thirty years younger than Ed. She said she was a hairstylist before marrying Ed."

"Do you know how they met?"

Benny smiled. "She was hitchhiking. He picked her up."

"So that rumor is true," Cheyenne said, smiling.

"That's what Ed told me, much to Terri's horror. She tried to turn it into this cute RomCom-like moment. She had a knack for reimagining events in her life."

"What brought Ed to Costa Rica?"

"Y2K."

"Ed North was one of those who thought Y2K would trigger the end of the world?" Cheyenne asked.

"I told you before, he was eccentric," Benny said, grinning. "He bought a small farm near the Panama border, which he stocked with supplies for the end of the world. Y2K came and went without even a whimper, but Ed's love for Costa Rica didn't dissipate. It only kept growing. He bought a house closer to civilization in Atenas. I came into his life through his accountant, who is a friend and introduced us. I did some legal work for him. Small projects at first: setting up a couple corporations for him and doing some legal due-diligence work for him. Then he found that large farm near Mariposa Beach and he fell in love with it. I handled the legal work and closing for him, much to Terri's chagrin; she hated the land and did not want to move to Costa Rica or spend much time here."

"I heard that Costa Rica had become a source of friction in the marriage," Cheyenne said.

"Ed told me they were having problems even before that. I didn't ask too many questions about his personal life. I'm not a marriage counselor. Terri came down to Costa Rica maybe three times, then it was just Ed coming here alone. Within a year, he was coming down every month, usually flew down himself on his Cessna Skylane airplane. He called his trips down here Terri breaks. He was, um... a womanizer when he was down here without Terri."

"That dirty dog," Dana said.

"Ed said Terri didn't care as long as he kept his womanizing in Costa Rica only as to not embarrass her."

"Then he met Gracie Robles, and that all changed, right?" Cheyenne said.

Benny looked surprised. "You know about Gracie?"

"I've been interviewing her for the podcast. Met with her a couple days ago."

"Wow, Dana said you were good. I'm impressed. Ed kept her on the down-low, not wanting to get Terri on the warpath."

Dana jokingly raised her hand. "Who the heck is Gracie Robles?"

"Ed's serious girlfriend. According to Gracie, they were in love. She told me Ed was getting ready to divorce Terri. Sell most of his American assets and move down to Costa Rica full time and marry Gracie," Cheyenne said.

"Ed told me that as well. He said he was getting the paperwork going so he could divorce Terri when he got back to Florida. He was hoping to move down here, permanently, by the end of the year."

"What year was that?" Cheyenne asked.

"The year he disappeared," Benny said.

"Terri said he was flying down here and he never came back."

"Hard to believe. He always told me when he would be in

town so I could be ready for him. When he left, he told me he wouldn't be back for two or three months while he got the ball rolling on his divorce from Terri," Benny said.

"Terri claims that's not true. He wasn't planning on divorcing her. Their marriage was fine. She let him come down here once a month to live like a bachelor, but he was happy and ready to come home to her in Miami after a couple weeks of that," Cheyenne said.

"Like I said before, Terri has a knack for reimagining and bending reality to fit a narrative that makes her look best."

"Do you think Terri had anything to do with Ed's disappearance?"

"I have no proof of it, but yes, I do. I think Terri killed Ed because he was going to divorce her for another younger woman. Teri would get a piece of his estate, but not all of it. She seemed to me to be someone who wanted to continue living like a rich housewife of Miami Beach. She wouldn't be able to do that if Ed left her. Especially if he left her for Gracie Robles. That would rub salt in the wound for her."

"That's probably why she wanted to stop the podcast. Not just because I might have discovered what really happened to Ed, but because it would be too much of a blow to her ego if it was confirmed that he was planning to leave her for another woman," Cheyenne said.

"And then she turns up dead, but why?" Dana asked.

"That's the sixty-four-thousand-dollar question," Cheyenne replied.

Chapter Twenty-Four

THE NEXT DAY, Benny and Dana agreed to meet Cheyenne at Soda Linda for lunch. Benny wasn't sure it was a good idea for the three of them to be seen together at Mariposa Beach. But Dana insisted they had nothing to hide, so let the town gossip away.

Soda Linda was a counter-service-only diner at the other end of Main Street's Little Ark, which was the more popular hotspot for tourists and locals. Ark Row had the shops that catered to tourists—like Dana's bookstore and Big Mike's Surf Shop. The popular Qué Vista Restaurant and the only bar in town, The Giggling Dorado, were located across the street in Ark Row. But Soda Linda was farther down the street from all that, near the city limits into Mariposa Beach. Delicious food that catered to the locals was their specialty.

Out front, Dana and Benny were waiting for Cheyenne, who showed up in her Suzuki Jimny rental. Cheyenne parked in one of the spots in front of the diner. All three of them looked around like they were getting to rob the place. It felt awkward for Benny to be out and about. Dana could see that in his face.

"Maybe we should make it to go and head back to Casa Verde," Dana said.

"No, you're right. We've done nothing wrong, so we don't have to hide around," Benny said.

"Okie dokie," Dana said. It was Benny that would be the magnet for attention and whispering since they'd arrested him as a person of interest in Terri's murder.

It was midafternoon and the clouds were dark as they threatened a downpour, so the open-air diner was empty. The unlikely trio sat down on the stools. The diner was typical of the *sodas* found throughout Costa Rica, small food stands that dotted the beach towns up and down the coast. The oval-shaped diner was poured from cement down to the very stools, so it wasn't the comfiest of spots, but the food was to die for. Like most mom-and-pop sodas in Costa Rica, Soda Linda was a family affair. Linda Orozco owned it with her husband, Nestor, and her son, Oscar, worked with his parents, serving delicious meals to the locals and tourists. They served typical Tico cuisine: casados, Gallo pinto, picadillo de papa, platano maduro.

Linda greeted them warmly.

"Glad to see the OIJ came to their senses and released you," Nestor Orozco said as he shook Benny's hand vigorously.

"Nestor, I'm sure he doesn't want to talk about that," Linda said, swatting her hubby lightly with a dish towel.

Benny smiled. "It's okay, just glad to be back at Mariposa Beach. And we're starving."

"You've come to the right place then, my friend," Nestor said. He looked at Cheyenne curiously, giving her an "and-you-are?" look.

Dana did the introductions, telling them that Cheyenne was a podcaster, and why she was in town.

"It's really you? I love your podcast," an excited Oscar said, nudging his dad over so he could meet Cheyenne face-to-face.

"Thank you. It's always fun meeting fans of the podcast."

"I have a podcast on all day while cooking at the soda. Makes the day go much faster," Oscar said.

"Okay, that's enough, you two, let our guests eat. They're starving," Linda said, shooing her husband and Oscar away from Cheyenne.

Dana ordered a chicken casado, while Benny ordered the fish casado.

"So what exactly is a casado?" Cheyenne asked.

"It's a staple dish in Costa Rica. It's rice, black beans, plantains, salad, and tortillas. You get a protein choice of chicken, beef, or fish. Unless you're a vegetarian, then you can skip the protein," Dana explained.

"I'm a recovering vegan, not doing that again," Cheyenne said, smiling. The menu was written on a chalkboard. She looked at it for a few seconds, not recognizing most of the dishes served. "Well, that casado sounds delicious. I'll have one of those too with fish, please," Cheyenne said.

"Coming right up," Linda said as she got to work.

"Something that's bugging me about his mess," Dana said while they waited for their food.

"What's that?" Cheyenne asked.

"Burt seemed to know a lot about the case."

"He's the victim's husband. It makes sense they would keep him in the loop of any development in the case," Benny said.

"I don't know how the police conduct their investigations here, but in the States the police are notorious for keeping most details of an active investigation close to their chest. Not sharing much information, even with the frustrated family members," Cheyenne said.

"And you said the spouse is usually the prime suspect in these types of murders?" Dana asked.

"It is back in the States," Cheyenne said.

They stopped talking about murder when their meals arrived. They hungrily dug in, washing down the deliciousness with freshly made pineapple juice.

They had just finished eating when they heard a vehicle braking hard. All three of them turned around to see a black Nissan Armada. Burt Kaminski climbed out. *Oh boy*, Dana thought. As far as Burt was concerned, even though Benny hadn't been charged with a crime, the police had arrested him as a person of interest in his wife's murder. And there he was, enjoying a meal alfresco.

"I heard they let you out," Burt said, walking up to the three.

"That's because he's innocent," Dana said.

Benny put his hand on her arm as if to say, *Don't engage.*

Cheyenne sprang into action. She jumped from the stool, digging out her handheld recorder from her bag. She walked right up to Burt and shoved the recorder in his face.

"Mr. Kaminski, can I ask you a few questions about your wife's death and Ed North's disappearance?"

Burt looked at Cheyenne and the recorder in her hand like a deer in the headlights.

"No comment," he said as he jumped back in his car. Before he drove off, he lowered the passenger-side window, leaned over and shouted, "You better hide your tire irons around that fella." He took off before anyone could say anything else.

"That was uncalled for," Dana said.

"He just lost his wife, so I'm sure there is a lot of raw emotion he's dealing with," Benny said, sounding more empathic toward the man who had just called him a killer than Dana had been.

"Did you really think he would grant you an interview on the spot?" Dana asked Cheyenne.

"No, but I figured my recorder would send him running off to the hills," Cheyenne said with a grin.

"Well played," Dana replied with a wide smile.

"I think we better head back. I should lie low at home until this case is resolved," Benny said, sounding crestfallen.

"Of course," Dana said.

Benny and Dana had walked to the soda, so Cheyenne drove them back to Casa Verde. Benny sat in the back. Dana was in the front passenger seat. She looked out the window as a thought kept crawling through her head about Burt Kaminski. Then it hit her. "Oh, that son of a biscuit," Dana said out loud.

"What is it?" Cheyenne asked.

"I need to make a call. If I'm right..." Dana trailed off, looking back out the window. Benny and Cheyenne looked at her, puzzled, as she grabbed her phone and made a call.

Chapter Twenty-Five

It had been almost two days since the weird encounter between Burt and Dana, Benny, and Cheyenne. Shirley Pacheco had flown back to the city. Benny preferred to stay either at his place or with Dana at Casa Verde. The Mariposa Beach community had rallied behind Benny; even the cynical, see-the-worst-in-everything leader of the Gossip Brigade, Doña Amada, had told Benny it was laughable to think he would have the gumption to kill anyone, let alone two people. It sounded like a backhanded compliment, but at least she wouldn't be spreading around rumors about his involvement in Ed North's and Terri's untimely demises.

Dana's phone rang. She smiled, having been waiting for this call. She picked it up, looking at Benny and mouthing off to him: *Burt Kaminski.*

Burt didn't bother with hellos. He got right to it.

"I just got off the phone with my lawyer. What's this business about a long-lost will from Ed North you supposedly found?"

"We've been through the reams of documents amassed in Benny's legal practice over the years. And in one of the last

142

banker's boxes that was searched, we found Ed's old will. Properly signed and notarized."

"I would love to see this supposed will," Burt said.

"There is only the one copy. And with his lawyers back in the city, we want to hand-deliver it. So we're going up to the city tomorrow morning. Until then, we don't feel comfortable taking a picture of it or emailing it, which is why we're driving it up there tomorrow. Your lawyer can call Shirley Pacheco tomorrow afternoon, when you can see it. Until then, this bad boy isn't leaving our side, sorry."

"Can you at least give the gist of this supposed will?" Burt asked.

"The will was pretty clear. Ed's estate was to be divided equally among his three children. A generous cash amount for Terri, but the bulk of his estate was left to his children."

"Hard to believe," Burt said.

"I guess that will be up to a judge to decide. What will you do if it's validated?"

"If it's proven to be authentic in a court of law, then I would respect that. I'm not about to get into a legal battle with the kids, especially with Terri now gone," Burt said.

"Just like that, huh?" Dana said, not really believing Burt would just walk away from Ed's fortune.

"If that's the way the cookie crumbles, I would. I respect the law. Always have," Burt said.

Dana was impressed with how well he was taking the news. She imagined Terri's reaction would have been nothing short of nuclear annihilation if she were still alive.

"More fodder for that podcast, I suppose," Burt added.

"Cheyenne Lively is coming over to my place to interview Benny for the podcast. At first, he was hesitant to talk to her, but she's won him over and was willing to talk to her, especially after finding Ed's will, and will be telling her everything he knows."

"Well, isn't that just grand?" Burt said sarcastically before hanging up.

Cheyenne and Nick Suárez arrived at Casa Verde at five p.m. They had dinner, then Nick spent thirty minutes setting up his equipment.

"Nervous?" Cheyenne asked Dana.

"A little."

"I'm still not sure this is such a great idea," Benny said.

"It could finally put an end to all this unpleasantness for you, Benny," Dana said.

"But at what cost?" Benny asked. He looked over at Cheyenne with an accusatory glance. Dana understood his apprehension and discomfort, but she was confident that this was the best course of action in order to finally clear Benny's name.

It was pitch-dark at nine p.m. The utter darkness that enveloped Casa Verde was something that still took Dana by surprise, even though she was nearing her first-year anniversary of moving to Mariposa Beach. The urban jungles she had lived on before moving to Mariposa Beach didn't really go quiet and dark. Casa Verde was nestled in a literal jungle setting. It was peaceful and beautiful even in the darkness, but there was also an eeriness to the tranquility of that dark stillness where the loudest noises came from the howler monkeys and the crickets.

A block away from Casa Verde, a car drove down the rutted road and parked. A figure exited the vehicle and crept along the wall of the property. The person was dressed in black and carried a large black duffle bag, melting into the pitch-blackness. It became a shadow walking toward the tall concrete wall surrounding Casa Verde. To prevent burglars from jumping over it, the top of the wall was adorned with barbed wire and broken glass embedded into the concrete. It was a common sight in Costa Rica. The little Central American country whose motto was *pura vida*—pure life—might be peaceful, but break-ins and burglary were a constant worry, especially in the rural beach communities like Mariposa Beach, where the closest police station was a tiny substation over ten miles away. Residents protected their homes as much as possible, hoping to deter the crooks from trying. But the shadow seemed determined as it made its way down the wall of the property.

Casa Verde sat on the pathway leading from the Tranquil Bay Resort to Mariposa Beach. A wrought-iron side door provided convenient quick access to the pathway as an alternative to going all the way down the long gravel driveway in front of the house. The shadow stopped at the metal door and looked around, then put the bag on the ground and removed something from it. A moment later, a blue hue and a few sparks fluttered in the darkness with the sound of a crackle ricocheting from the trees. It only took a minute for the shadow to make its way inside Casa Verde through the side-gate door. The shadow quickly made its way to the main house like a panther stalking its prey. The lights inside Casa Verde were on as Dana, Benny, Cheyenne, and Nick worked on the podcast. The black shadow smiled at the sight. All its problems would soon be wiped out in one single swoop.

The shadow reached the large cylinder-shaped propane tank that many homes in Costa Rica had in the absence of a gas line coming from a street public utility. The cylinder tank abutted the house, so the shadow moved slowly and low to the ground to avoid detection. Once at the tank, the shadow removed a gas container from the bag, then made its way around the wall of the house. It walked back toward the propane gas cylinder, pouring a trail of gasoline from the house to the tank and splashing the rest all around the cylinder. Satisfied with its handiwork, the black shadow went to the side door leading out to the pathway. At about the halfway point, the black shadow stopped, and once again it reached inside the duffle bag and removed several bottles and a box of long fireplace matches. The black shadow pulled out one of the heavyweight premium matches from the box and was about to strike it when the pitch-darkness dissipated in an instant into a bright light that turned the night into day.

Chapter Twenty-Six

BEFORE THE NIGHT sky turned to light on the black shadow, Dana, Benny, Cheyenne, and Nick had been glued to a computer monitor, watching every step the shadow took.

The video was coming from the multiple night-vision cameras Nick had set up around the Casa Verde property—inside and outside.

He had rigged two cameras on a tree across from Casa Verde to capture the pathway in both directions. It was the perfect spot for the devices; his only concern was that one of the always curious howler monkeys would find the cameras and mess with them. Luckily, the monkeys were busy howling at the moon from other trees.

Dana already had a video doorbell system installed at the front gate, so they were set in that direction. But everyone agreed that if there were to be a visitor that night, as they suspected, it wouldn't come through the front gate. After monitoring the cameras for a couple of hours, one of the cameras hidden in a tree across from Dana's property picked up some suspicious activity.

"They're here," Dana said, impersonating the eerie tone of that little girl from the movie *Poltergeist*.

Everyone crowded around the monitor to watch the show unfolding right before their eyes. Gathered around Nick, who was manning the video equipment, were Dana, Benny, Cheyenne, and OIJ detective Gabriela Rojas.

"There's a car coming down the road," Nick said.

"With its lights off. That's not suspicious," Benny added.

Gabriela leaned to watch what was unfolding right outside of Dana's property's walls.

The car stopped a few feet from Dana's property. The group watched as the driver-side door opened and someone dressed in black, head to toe, got out of the car.

"Son of a gun is wearing a complete face covering," Gabriela said.

"Looks like a ski mask," Cheyenne said.

"Where do you even get a ski mask in the tropics?" Dana asked.

They all watched the black-clad figure open the trunk, removing a large bag from it.

All eyes were glued to the computer monitor where Nick had set up a gallery of eight video feeds for each camera that he had hidden outside and inside Casa Verde. The shadow figure came down the pathway and then tucked in close to Dana's property outside wall. It walked along the wall, hugging it like an inmate on a prison break trying to avoid the search lights.

When the shadow got to the side steel door, they saw it stop and place the bag on the ground as it removed something, although they could not tell what the shadow had in its hand because of the darkness.

"Is that a gun?" a worried Benny said, staring at the screen.

They saw the shadow squat low next to the door, then they saw a light of blue hue and sparks flying into the air.

"That's a handheld welding machine," Nick said, sounding impressed. It took only about a minute for the shadow to breach the side door and gain access to the property.

"Oh my gosh," Dana said with her hand to her mouth. The blanket of security she felt at home had been ripped off in an instant.

Benny put his arm around her. They continued watching the surreal event unfolding before their eyes as this masked person was creeping along inside Dana's property.

"I'm glad we told Ramón and Carmen to stay put in their home tonight no matter what they might see or hear," Dana said as she watched the shadow slowly make its way to the main house, prancing on its feet like a demented ballet dancer. They saw the shadow stop as it riffled through its bag once again, this time pulling out what looked like a gasoline can.

Gabriela rose to her feet, watching as the shadow tipped the can to spill out its liquid content.

"Is that gasoline?" an incredulous Cheyenne asked.

"Looks that way," Benny said.

Then they watched the shadow walking backward toward the propane cylinder, splashing a trail of gasoline between the house and the cylinder.

"Holy moly! He's trying to blow up the propane tank," Dana said.

"And burn down the house," Benny added.

"With us inside," Cheyenne said. It was the first time Dana had detected a trace of fear in the spunky podcaster's voice.

They were under strict radio silence to ensure the shadow couldn't hear them communicating via the device. She pressed the handheld radio button once. One squelch meant for the other police officers hiding nearby to get ready to pounce.

The shadow stopped at the propane cylinder, where it seemed to splash more gasoline all around it. The shadow then picked up its bag and headed back toward the side door, stopping halfway between the door to its escape and the propane tank.

"I think it's time to put an end to this, Detective Rojas," Benny said nervously.

"Just another few seconds," Rojas said, her eyes glued to the monitor, her right hand white-knuckling the radio.

The shadow reached back to its bag of evil tricks and removed what looked like a bottle and something else. The group watched as the shadow removed a long stick from the box.

"That's a match," an anxious Benny said.

"That must be...a Molotov cocktail," Cheyenne said, mouth agape.

"Good heavens," Dana said.

That was enough for Rojas. She pressed the radio button three times, singling Juan Picado, who was outside with several police officers waiting to spring into action. Within a second of Rojas's signal, Picado had ordered the other officers to turn on their police floodlights, plucking the shadow out of its protective darkness as Rojas ran outside with the rest of the gang following her closely—with Dana leading the pack in a mad dash.

Rojas told everyone to stay back, but no one listened as they ran outside where the police officers already had the shadow in custody.

Even with the ski mask over its face, the shadow's look was priceless. All they could see were its eyes, which were wide as they darted around at everyone gathering around. A literal deer-in-headlights look.

Rojas walked up to the shadow, and she removed the ski mask. The color in Burt Kaminski's face had drained. He looked like death warmed over. Dana looked down and saw three bottles with a cloth sticking out of the bottles' necks, serving as a wicker. A box of matches dropped at Burt's feet, with several long matches used for fireplaces strewn about the ground. Dana looked up, dumbfounded. Burt looked at her with rage.

"Let me guess. There is no Ed North mystery will you found," Burt said.

"Nope," Dana said. "All this mayhem for what? Some money?"

"It's a lot of money," Burt said with a smirk.

Cheyenne stuck her recorder in his face again, but this time, he couldn't run off into his car. "Why did you try to blow up Dana's house with us inside, Mr. Kaminski? Why did you try to kill us tonight?"

"Ask that little tomato over there. She seems to have figured it all out," Burt said.

Dana looked at Benny. "Little tomato? Did I just time-warp to the fifties?" Benny smiled.

"This little tomato just hoodwinked you into those handcuffs," Dana said. "I figured you were behind all this chaos but couldn't really figure out why you went through all this if you were already enjoying the money by having married Terri. So I asked Cheyenne to do some checking up on you and Terri in the Florida courts and sure enough, Terri had just filed divorce papers on you. Cheyenne also found that monster ironclad prenup you signed before you married Terri, so you were going to be cut off from Ed North's money," Dana said.

"I also talked with Terri's sister, who told me you were the one pushing Terri to fly down to Mariposa Beach to stop the podcast. But you didn't care about the podcast, did you? You wanted her out here so you could kill her and pin the murder on Benny," Cheyenne said.

Burt didn't respond; he just shrugged.

"But then you slipped up when we talked at the resort, didn't you? It didn't dawn on me until the other night. You knew my brake line was cut. How the heck did you know that? I didn't tell you. I asked Gabriela. She said they didn't share that tidbit with you either."

Burt said nothing, so Dana answered for him. "You knew, because *you* cut my brake line, didn't you?"

"You also had made it clear this was your first visit to Costa Rica, but I checked with customs. You were here once before," Rojas said.

"Let me guess. Burt was down here the week Ed North disappeared," Benny said.

"Bingo," Dana said.

"And now the police caught you red-handed, trying to kill us all. What went through that evil little head of yours? You wipe us all out and the case and the podcast are over? Your life goes back to like it was before?" Dana said.

"Everything was working out perfectly, if it weren't for your meddling," Kaminski said, glaring at Dana.

"You thought I would just let you frame, Benny for your crimes?" Dana said.

"I'm not saying anything else. If you're taking me to jail, just do it," Burt said.

"My pleasure," Rojas said, nodding at the police officers, who dragged Burt away into a police van.

"What happens now?" Dana asked Gabriela.

"We'll conduct our investigation and turn it over to the prosecutor. But don't worry, I can guarantee you Burt Kaminski won't be set free. He'll be put into preventive detention until the trial starts, and with the mountain of evidence collected today, he won't get out anytime soon."

Chapter Twenty-Seven

A MONTH later

Dana was getting ready to go for a run when she received a notification on her phone announcing a new episode of the *What Really Happened* podcast. *It's showtime*, Dana thought.

Dana felt her heart flutter, and the butterflies in her stomach were going wild as she opened the podcast app and queued up the first episode.

How many true crime podcasts had she consumed over the years? Too many to keep track of, but now for this podcast was different. The *true* in *true crime* was her truth. Benny's truth. The entire Mariposa Beach community's truth. Casa Verde would be front and center. Cheyenne had promised that they should talk about the details of that night in a way so as not to dox her. The last thing she wanted was to become a macabre tourist hotspot. She could imagine tourists in town saying, *After a swim in the ocean and hanging out on the beach, let's go check out that house that was almost blown up.*

Dana was most worried that everything she and Benny had gone through would be on that podcast. And millions of true crime fans that listened to Cheyenne's podcast would mop all of it up like bread in olive oil.

Dana felt a lump in her throat as she walked out to her veranda and plopped down on her favorite lounge chair next to a sprawled-out Wally, who had taken over the chair and, as usual, he wasn't budging as Dana tried to sit down.

"Don't be greedy now, Wally. Plenty of room for both of us," Dana said. Wally hardly moved. "An inch, give me an inch."

Wally yawned, looking at her squinty-eyed, and plopped back to sleep without giving her half an inch. Dana scrunched over in the corner and she plopped the earbuds in as she hit play on the phone's podcast app. The ominous theme music kicked in creepily, slowly increasing the suspense into a sudden decrescendo as the theme song faded to the background and Cheyenne's silky voice took over.

Hello, true crime fiends. This is your intrepid host, Cheyenne Lively of the What Really Happened *True Crime Podcast. We're back from hiatus and, as usual, I have an amazing true crime tale to tell. It starts with the disappearance of eccentric multimillion-aire Ed North in paradise.*

Beautiful Mariposa Beach, Costa Rica. This one has it all: an exotic tropical setting of white-sand beaches and warm ocean water blue as topaz. A rainforest teeming with wildlife like the adorable howling monkeys, iguanas the size of Godzilla, and, of course, the human condition: love, affairs, marriage, divorce, murder, greed, an innocent man being framed and falsely arrested, and the attempted murder of yours truly.

That's right, my true crime fiends. There was an attempt made on my life just for trying to bring you this podcast. So make sure you

*subscribe and leave a review for it on your favorite podcasting
app. And make sure to support our sponsors, which pays the bills
around here. It's the least you could do for me, almost getting
blown up for all you true crime fiends out there.*

*So buckle up, my fiends, because this case is a doozy. I have a lot
to cover in the next six episodes, which will air on Wednesdays.
So sit back and listen to What Really Happened to Ed North, my
true crime fiends.*

Dana smiled as she listened. It was surreal listening to
Cheyenne's warm radio voice this time since they had met and
gone through so much the last couple of months. Cheyenne was
no longer just a voice of a popular podcast; she considered her a
friend. Dana clicked the share function on the app to send a link
to the podcast to Benny via text. He texted her back right away:
Already listening with a smiling emoji.

For the next six weeks, they released a new podcast episode as
Dana, Benny, and just about everyone else in Mariposa Beach
tuned in. Despite being fodder for the podcast, Dana and Benny
enjoyed it, but not the fifteen minutes of fame that it brought
them. It had blown up, even beating Joe Rogan for a couple
weeks to take the number one spot as the most popular podcast
on the charts. Cheyenne had another smash hit under her belt.
And the truths she had dug up about the night when Burt tried
to blow up Casa Verde were jaw-dropping.

From the podcast, Dana learned the scary details of the
night Burt broke into Casa Verde and the items in Burt's bag of
evil tricks as he tried to burn down the house with them all
inside.

Burt had been able to break into Dana's property so easily because of the expertise he'd picked up in two previous professions before selling cars: one as a welder, the other as a cat burglar. He had even done some time in Ohio for burglarizing homes, so breaking and entering was old hat to him. The side door was no match against an experienced burglar and welder armed with a battery-powered handheld portable welding machine. Also in his bag of goodies was a gasoline can, which he had spray-painted black so it, too, would blend into the darkness of the night, and three bottles of Imperial beer filled with kerosene and turned into Molotov cocktails. The liquid he poured around Dana's house and the propane cylinder were indeed gasoline.

Burt's obvious nefarious plan was to light the torch and toss the Molotov cocktails at the propane cylinder, the gasoline trail leading up to the house, and against the gas-soaked wall of the house to create a massive propane-tank explosion that would have leveled the house and killed everyone inside while he slithered back to his rental car.

The police later found out that he had already checked out of the Tranquil Bay Resort. His luggage was being held by the bellhop. He had booked a first-class seat on the six fifteen a.m. flight from San José to Miami. Burt's plan after having killed four more people was to pick up his luggage, drive to the airport and wait for his early flight back to the States.

In prison, he confessed to killing Terri after he confronted her about her divorce plans. She not only confirmed them but demanded he move out of the resort that night, saying that she was kicking him out of their posh Miami Beach home, and that with the ironclad prenup he was getting nothing. He wasn't about to start over in his sixties without money or a home. Especially after everything he had done for her. Burt claimed he had been having an affair with Terri and she was the one who asked him to get rid of Ed North before he divorced her—an irony that angered Burt even more after she planned to divorce him.

Whether Terri was really in cahoots with killing her first husband was up to debate by her sister, who insisted Burt was lying about her involvement. The sister told Cheyenne that she believed Burt wanted to get rid of Ed so he could marry Terri and enjoy Ed's vast fortune. A plan that worked for years before Terri decided she wanted a divorce, sealing her fate.

Not that it mattered anymore, but Dana was pretty sure Terri was involved in the planning of Ed's demise. She just had Burt do the dirty work.

The biggest mystery of Burt's evildoing was how he was able to plant the murder weapon in Benny's safe. The answer came once again from his cat-burglar days and a rare earth hockey puck magnet. It was a powerful magnet that allowed Burt to open Benny's electronic safe in mere seconds without damage or sign of entry so he could plant the tire iron inside and lock the safe back up as if nothing had happened. Burt knew about the safe because Terri had mentioned it to him. Benny had made the mistake of showing Ed his safe before he vanished since he wanted a hidden safe in the floor of his house.

The fact that Burt had been so well prepared with a portable welding machine, the magnet, even the ski mask—a rarity in the tropics—led the police to believe he had come to the country to kill Terri and frame Benny. So his claims of having snapped when Terri told him about her divorce plans seemed quite bogus.

They officially cleared Benny as a suspect and person of interest in the disappearance of Ed North and the murder of Terri Kaminski. As to what had happened to Ed? Burt had flown to Costa Rica and just as he had sneaked into Casa Verde, he had done the same in Ed's farmhouse. After the dastardly deed was done, he took Ed's deep-sea fishing boat far into the ocean, where he dumped the weighted body into the Pacific Ocean to be lost forever. He then flew back to Florida and continued his courtship of Terri, eventually marrying into all that money.

The supposed old will Dana found was just bait that worked perfectly to catch Burt in the act. However, since Burt was looking at spending a few decades in a Costa Rican prison and Terri was dead, Benny speculated that Ed's kids would finally have access to their stolen inheritance.

The success of the podcast led to a media frenzy. Dana and Benny had gotten interview requests from Dateline and 20/20 to go over their ordeal. Even a Netflix producer had reached out, looking to cash in on the success of the podcast with their own documentary about the case. Dana and Benny were unsure how to proceed with those requests. Life had just gotten back to the peace and quiet of slow-paced Mariposa Beach. It was why Dana had moved there. She wasn't too keen to relive everything that had happened over and over again with all the different network shows out there eager to have their own version of the podcast on their networks. None of that sounded too appealing to Dana, especially at that moment, when she and Benny were enjoying a swim.

Dana found herself surprised to actually miss hanging around with fellow journalist Cheyenne. They had made a good team. She also felt a tinge of jealousy about Cheyenne's success as a true crime podcaster, but those feelings quickly dissipated as she floated in the warm waters of the Pacific Ocean in Benny's arms.

That evening, after their ocean swim, Dana was at home, waiting for Benny so they could go to dinner. He texted her that he was at the front gate.

Dana heard tires crunching gravel and the headlights coming up the driveway. She stepped outside to greet him. It perplexed her that the vehicle seemed smaller than Benny's truck. It looked like a Jeep. Dana wondered if Benny had bought a new car. As he pulled up to the front of the house under the carport's bright lights, she saw Benny wasn't driving his truck or new car. He was in a cherry-red mint 1940s Jeep Willys. "No way," Dana said, smiling ear to ear.

Benny parked and got out of the vehicle with a smile as wide as Dana's.

"Is that really... It is Big Red!" Dana squealed like a teenager.

She ran down her front steps toward Big Red, restored back to its glory.

"Gabriela said the police still needed Big Red for trial," Dana said, walking around her beloved Jeep.

"I asked her to fib a little so I could surprise you," Benny said.

"Oh, you rascals."

"Here you go, darling," Benny said, holding up the keys.

"Thank you, thank you, thank you," Dana said, taking the keys, then hugging and kissing Benny.

She jumped into the driver's seat. They had completely restored Big Red. "She looks amazing," Dana said. She fired her up and smiled as Big Red's engine purred.

"Hop on, good-looking," Dana said.

Benny smiled as he climbed into the passenger seat and Dana revved the engine.

"Oh, boy," Benny said, making the sign of the cross. He

wrapped his hand around the front grab handle. "Take it easy, hon, she just got out of the shop."

"Of course," Dana said with a devilish grin.

"Where are we going?" a nervous Benny asked.

"Off-roading," Dana said, putting the pedal to the metal. She drove Big Red like a horse jockey off to the races, pulling out of Casa Verde towards the lush mountains that surrounded Mariposa Beach.

Language Notes

Doña - In Spanish-speaking countries, like Costa Rica, "doña" is often used as a title of respect for a woman along with her first name, hence Doña Dana.

Don - Just like "doña", but for males. So, Don Benny.

Tico is an idiomatic term used for a native of Costa Rica. Costa Ricans are usually called ticos by themselves as well as by people of other Spanish-speaking countries. This comes from the Costa Rican tendency to add the diminutive "tico" to the end of words. For example, when saying something is small would be "chico" in Spanish— Costa Ricans would say it is "chiquitico."

Pura Vida - direct English translation is "pure life." The phrase is used for many things: to say hello, goodbye, to express happiness, good news and so on.

Pulperia - a small convenience store equivalent to a Cornershop or a NYC bodega.

Casa Verde - direct English translation is "green house." The nickname given to Dana's home because of its lush green surroundings.

Check out Lonely Planet's Costa Rican Spanish Phrasebook & Dictionary to learn more about Tico Spanish phrases and vocabulary.

What's Next

Thank you for reading this book! I hope you enjoyed it. If so, please let other cozy mystery fans know by leaving a short review on Amazon. Reviews help spread the word about these books.

You can also follow me on Amazon and BookBub to be notified by them of new releases. Go to **www.KCAmes/Links**.

Make sure to join my mailing list to be notified when the next book in this series is available and to download my Costa Rica Cookbook for free over at **www.KCAmes.com/Subscribe**

About the Author

I was born and raised in Costa Rica, but now live in San Francisco, California.

I've always loved cozy mysteries, so when I decided to write my cozy mysteries, I just knew I had to base it in my home country of Costa Rica.

That's how this beach cozy mystery series came about. I'm excited to bring you more cozy mysteries set in the Pacific Coast of Costa Rica.
You can learn more about me and my books over at my website: www.KCAmes.com.

Sign up for my newsletter for book updates, animal pics, and my recipe book of traditional Costa Rica dishes, for free:

kcames.com/subscribe

Connect with me on Social Media...

facebook.com/kcamesmysteries
twitter.com/kcamesbooks
goodreads.com/kcames

Also by K.C. Ames